"I'm not looking for a personal relationship with you.

"I don't have time for flirting or any of that nonsense. I need a skilled assistant. That's all."

Jenna fought to hang on to her temper. Fighting for control, she studied the man, allowing her gaze to slide over him from his curls to his rather large feet. Eventually she raised her eyes to meet his and said, "Tell me, Sir Ian, are you always this obnoxious or did I luck out and catch you on a bad day? I can't for the life of me imagine why you think that I—or any other self-respecting woman, for that matter— would be interested in having a relationship with you."

He looked startled for a moment, then gave her a boyish grin that was wholly unexpected…and devastatingly attractive. "You'll do, Ms. Craddock. You'll do."

Dear Reader,

Well, the new year is upon us—and if you've resolved to read some wonderful books in 2004, you've come to the right place. We'll begin with *Expecting!* by Susan Mallery, the first in our five-book MERLYN COUNTY MIDWIVES miniseries, in which residents of a small Kentucky town find love—and scandal—amidst the backdrop of a midwifery clinic. In the opening book, a woman returning to her hometown, pregnant and alone, finds herself falling for her high school crush—now all grown up and married to his career! Or so he thinks....

Annette Broadrick concludes her SECRET SISTERS trilogy with *MacGowan Meets His Match.* When a woman comes to Scotland looking for a job *and* the key to unlock the mystery surrounding her family, she finds both—with the love of a lifetime thrown in!—in the Scottish lord who hires her. In *The Black Sheep Heir,* Crystal Green wraps up her KANE'S CROSSING miniseries with the story of the town outcast who finds in the big, brooding stranger hiding out in her cabin the soul mate she'd been searching for.

Karen Rose Smith offers the story of an about-to-be single mom and the handsome hometown hero who makes her wonder if she doesn't have room for just one more male in her life, in *Their Baby Bond.* THE RICHEST GALS IN TEXAS, a new miniseries by Arlene James, in which three blue-collar friends inherit a million dollars—each!—opens with *Beautician Gets Million-Dollar Tip!* A hairstylist inherits that wad just in time to bring her salon up to code, at the insistence of the infuriatingly handsome, if annoying, local fire marshal. And in Jen Safrey's *A Perfect Pair,* a woman who enlists her best (male) friend to help her find her Mr. Right suddenly realizes he's right there in front of her face—i.e., said friend! Now all she has to do is convince *him* of this....

So bundle up, and happy reading. And come back next month for six new wonderful stories, all from Silhouette Special Edition.

Sincerely,

Gail Chasan
Senior Editor

Please address questions and book requests to:
Silhouette Reader Service
U.S.: 3010 Walden Ave., P.O. Box 1325, Buffalo, NY 14269
Canadian: P.O. Box 609, Fort Erie, Ont. L2A 5X3

MacGowan Meets His Match

ANNETTE BROADRICK

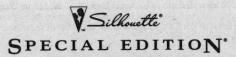

SPECIAL EDITION®

Published by Silhouette Books

America's Publisher of Contemporary Romance

This book is dedicated to Anna Vinson, a dear friend who had the nerve to leave Texas and move to Colorado.

I miss you. Thank goodness for e-mail and phone calls!

 SILHOUETTE BOOKS

ISBN 0-373-24586-6

MACGOWAN MEETS HIS MATCH

Visit Silhouette at www.eHarlequin.com

Printed in U.S.A.

Books by Annette Broadrick

ANNETTE BROADRICK

believes in romance and the magic of life. Since 1984, Annette has shared her view of life and love with readers. In addition to being nominated by *Romantic Times* as one of the Best New Authors of that year, she has also won the *Romantic Times* Reviewers' Choice Award for Best in its Series; the *Romantic Times* WISH Award; and the *Romantic Times* Lifetime Achievement Awards for Series Romance and Series Romantic Fantasy.

All underlined places are
fictitious.

Prologue

Sydney, Australia
Early February 2004

"Resigning! What do you mean you're resigning!" Jenna Craddock's employer sputtered. Basil Fitzgerald was a lovable bearlike man, happily married to the same woman for forty-five years. He was gruff and abrupt, his camouflage for a tender heart.

Jenna was going to miss him.

"Why would you leave a perfectly good position after six years? What do you want? More money? More holiday time? Talk to me!"

Jenna had known he would not be happy with her

announcement. She sat in front of his desk, her hands folded in her lap while she waited for him to stop blustering.

"My leaving has nothing to do with my position with you. It's a personal matter."

"Oh. You're getting married, huh?"

Jenna laughed. "Of course not. When have I had time to date with such a slave master as you?" she teased. "I'm moving to the U.K. I've been saving for years for the chance to return as an adult and explore."

"Fine. Then take a leave of absence and go. There's no reason to resign."

"I have no idea how long I might be gone. Once there, I may decide to stay. I don't want to leave here with you thinking I'll be back."

"Nonsense. You're an Australian. You can't expect to find work in another country without legal papers."

"Actually, I was born in Cornwall. I'm a citizen there."

"Really? You never mentioned that to me. I've always thought of you as a native Australian."

She smiled and didn't comment.

He studied her for several minutes in silence. "Come to think of it," he said finally, "I don't know much about you except that you've been an exceptional assistant and I'm going to miss your quiet efficiency. Maude thinks you hung the moon.

She tells me I've been much easier to live with since you've been with me, keeping me organized.''

"Don't worry. Personnel will find someone equally capable for you. I won't be leaving for another six weeks, which will give them plenty of time to find someone.''

"Hmph.''

She smiled. She would have been disappointed if he'd indicated that she could be easily replaced. "I'm not dropping off the edge of the earth, you know,'' she said gently. "I'll keep you informed about where I am and what I'm doing.''

Basil sighed. "Nothing I can say will change your mind, will it?''

"No, sir.''

"Well, if you don't find whatever it is you're looking for, you know you can always come back here.''

"Thank you.''

"Now I have to pass on this news to Maude. She'll be convinced that I've done something to drive you away.''

"Don't worry. I'll explain to your wife and make certain she knows this trip has nothing to do with you,'' Jenna replied with a grin.

When Jenna left his office, Basil stared sadly at the door she'd closed behind her. Jenna was leaving…not just his legal firm, not just Sydney, but Australia, as well.

She would be greatly missed.

Chapter One

Late March 2004

"Welcome to Heathrow and thank you for flying British Airways. We hope that you enjoyed your flight and that you will remember us the next time you plan to travel."

The disembodied voice from the public address system barely managed to get through to Jenna's fatigue-numbed brain. With a stop in Singapore, she had been traveling for almost twenty-two hours. She'd managed to doze or nap during the trip, but what she had experienced was far from restful sleep.

She cleared Customs and was looking for a ride to her hotel by six o'clock in the morning, local time. Jenna had no idea what time her internal clock thought it was and at the moment didn't care. All she wanted to do was find a bed and crash.

After two days and nights in London, Jenna was ready to embark on her adventure. She had told Basil the truth when she said she wanted to explore England. What she hadn't told him was that she hoped to find some relatives who still lived in Cornwall.

She wondered if family was as important to other people as it was to her. Being without anyone for most of her life provided a strong motivation for Jenna to search for family. Of course, being on her own had made her independent to some degree, but she used to dream of a time when she'd have a home of her own and lots of family around.

The car she had rented was small and economical…just what she needed. She intended to take her time driving west, stopping when she grew tired regardless of the time and in general enjoying her very open-ended holiday.

If she drove west far enough, she would end up in the village of St. Just in Cornwall where she and her parents had lived for the first five years of her life. She'd been fascinated in school with the British Isles and Cornwall. It was her home place, after all.

At one time her father's sister lived in the area. She hoped her aunt was still alive. She knew Aunt Morwenna would be surprised to see her after all these years.

Jenna spent her first night on the road at a village nestled in the rolling hills of County Devon. Its quiet pastoral tempo was a far cry from the fast pace of Sydney and London.

Before she went to bed that night she studied her well-worn map one more time. Cornwall jutted into the sea like a slightly bent finger.

The next day she found roads to follow that gave her glimpses of the sea. More than once she stopped at a lay-by and walked along the paths she found, thrilled to be here at last.

Jenna had no trouble finding a place to stay once she reached St. Just. Tom Elliott, the proprietor of a cozy inn, told her that they were getting a trickling of tourists at this time of year, so he had plenty of room for her.

She explained that she wasn't certain how long she would be staying there and when she returned to the front desk, she asked him about things to do in St. Just.

"Well, if you like to hike, there's plenty of hiking to be done. If you want to look for the stone circles, we have them, as well. There's the golf club for those who have time to play."

"What about jobs?"

He shrugged. "Depends. You'd have better luck finding decent wages if you look in Penzance. Many people living here work there. Are you thinking of settling in these parts?"

She laughed. "Oh, I have no plans at all, really. My family was from this area and I had an urge to see what it was like. If I like it, I might decide to stay.''

Tom nodded. ''Yes, Craddock is a Cornish name, all right.''

''I'm looking for my aunt Morwenna. She's a Craddock, but her married name is Hoskins. Do you know of her or of any other Craddocks still living in the area?''

''Not offhand, no. My wife and I moved here from London about five years ago to get away from the rush and lead a quieter life. Come summer, it's far from quiet around here, but we do enjoy it. You might check at the pub down the street for any Craddocks. Somebody may know of a family or two. Besides, they have decent food there. I often go there for lunch myself.''

''Thank you,'' she said, slipping her purse strap over her shoulder and heading down the street. Jenna wanted to check the local phone directory, but she was hungry and tired and decided that she'd have dinner at Tom's pub first.

She found the pub in the center of the village. Once inside, she took her meal and tea to one of the tables near the front. She entertained herself watching the locals as they stopped by after a day's work for a pint or two.

By the time she left the pub, night had cloaked the area. She returned to the small inn.

''How was your search?'' Tom asked with a smile when she walked into the lobby.

''I decided to wait until tomorrow.''

"I was thinking while you were gone and decided to check the phone directory. I didn't find a Hoskins, but I found a Craddock who lives up the road a ways. Perhaps you could call."

"A capital idea. May I use your phone?"

Tom moved the phone closer to her side of the counter and handed her the phone book. She looked up the number and dialed. When a woman answered, Jenna said, "Hello. I was wondering if you happen to know if Morwenna Hoskins lives in this area. She used to be a Craddock." When the woman hesitated, Jenna added, "I'm her niece from Australia and I've lost touch with the rest of the family."

"Ah. Well, I doubt very much Morwenna would mind my giving you directions to her place." The woman gave her detailed directions to the row house where Morwenna lived. "I don't know her very well, you understand. She keeps to herself."

"Well, thank you for your help," Jenna replied. When she hung up the phone she was dancing. "I've found her! Just like that. A phone call and there she is!"

Tom smiled at her exuberance. "That's good. You haven't been here a full day and already found some of your kin."

Jenna practically skipped up the stairs to her room. Her aunt hadn't been listed so she may not have a phone. But it didn't matter. She'd wait until midmorning tomorrow and visit her. Jenna could hardly wait to see her aunt's face when she identified herself.

She had a difficult time falling to sleep that night.

By the next morning, Jenna was filled with anticipation, although she was nervous, as well. This was the day that she had been waiting for all these years. She could feel her heart thumping.

Jenna found the place with no trouble. She pulled up in front of her aunt's row house and slowly got out of the car. She took a couple of deep breaths to relieve the constriction in her chest, then walked up to the door and knocked. When she heard no one stirring, she worried that her aunt might have moved. Wouldn't that be ironic after Jenna had come so far to see her?

Jenna knocked again and waited.

A female voice yelled, "I'll be there when I get there. Just hold on. And you'd better not be peddling anything because I'm not interested!" At her last words Morwenna Hoskins swung open the door. At least Jenna guessed this was her aunt, although seeing her didn't trigger any memories.

The years had not been kind to Morwenna. Jenna knew that she was in her fifties and yet she looked considerably older. Morwenna leaned on a cane and looked at her with suspicion.

"Well? What do you want?"

"I, uh, I mean, hello," Jenna said. "I'm not selling anything. Actually I came from Australia to find you. I'm your niece, Jenna."

Whatever reaction Jenna had expected, she hadn't thought she would be stared at with such distaste. Morwenna studied her without stepping back to invite Jenna inside. Instead, her aunt continued to stand in the doorway as though she had never heard of her.

Jenna didn't know what to say. Why wasn't her aunt more pleased to see her?

Finally, Morwenna spoke. "My niece? If you're from Australia you must be Hedra and Tristan's girl."

Jenna relaxed a little and smiled. "Yes. Yes, I am."

Morwenna scowled. "I told them and told them that nothing good was going to come of their moving halfway around the world. That's exactly what I told them. 'Nothing good will come of your move.' And I was right, wasn't I? They were there no more than two years before they were gone—swept away by floodwaters or some such fool thing. I always said they should have listened to me, but then, Tristan always thought he knew best about everything." She eyed Jenna warily. "So what do you want?"

Dismay swept over Jenna. "I, uh, I just came by to introduce myself. I'm afraid I don't have many memories of living in Cornwall, but since this was the place I was born, I came back to get to know the rest of my family."

Morwenna was shaking her head before Jenna stopped speaking. "You've had a wasted trip, then. You don't have family around here. I don't know where Tristan found you—he would never say—but it wasn't around here."

Jenna stared at Morwenna, thinking she had misunderstood her. "Found me?"

"It's like what I told that man from Edinburgh that came looking for you a few months ago...we're not blood relatives. Who knows where they got you? Hedra showed up here one day with a newborn, proud as she could be. Tristan was beaming from ear to ear. I warned them about taking somebody else's child to raise. You never can tell what's in the blood, you know. Why, someone unknown like that can grow up to be thief or a murderer or something worse."

Jenna stared at the woman, doubting her ears. Was the woman insane? What was she rattling on about...and what did Morwenna consider worse than murder?

"Am I understanding you correctly?" Jenna finally managed to say. This woman was shattering her world. "You're telling me I was adopted?"

"Are you deaf or something? Yes, that's what I'm telling you. You're adopted." Her eyes narrowed. "You didn't know, huh?"

"No. I had no idea."

"Well, somebody should've told you before now, to my way of thinking. I can remember when I got the news that Tristan was gone. That was an awful time for me. My only sibling and all. A terrible time. If he'd only listened to me, he might have been alive today." Morwenna made a face. "I was real put out with them people calling from Australia, wanting me to take you in. I told them I had eight of my own to raise and I certainly didn't need a seven-year-old underfoot, as well.''

Morwenna's words beat at Jenna as though each one was a stone aimed at her heart. She had no way to protect herself, nothing to say. So the authorities had attempted to find a member of her family to take her before placing her in an orphanage.

Jenna stared at the woman in horror. She had to get away. Thank goodness she hadn't been invited into the woman's home. She would have felt suffocated by her anger and cruelty.

Despite the shock of discovering she'd been adopted, she was fervently grateful that she was no kin to this woman.

''Thank you for clearing up my confusion,'' Jenna said quietly. ''You mentioned a man from Edinburgh asking about me. Could you give me his name?''

''That's been a few months ago. Let me think…I believe it started with a *D*. Something *D*…Davis, Dennis…no, that's not right.''

''Could you describe him?''

''Why? You thinking about looking him up? He said he was from Edinburgh but he didn't fool me. He had an American accent. No telling where he was from. Wait a minute. His name sounded French…Dumas! That's it. Something Dumas. I don't remember his first name. You look nothing like him, if that's what you're thinking. He has dark hair and eyes and he's tall.'' Morwenna flicked a glance up and down Jenna as though to emphasize her statement.

Jenna knew she was far from being tall, so she nodded her understanding. "I appreciate your help," she said, wanting to run while Morwenna was drawing breath and before she continued talking.

She turned and walked back to her car, her shoulders back and her chin up.

Only after she entered the pub where she'd eaten the night before did she realize that she was trembling. She vaguely recognized that she was in shock. She asked for a cup of tea and when it was ready she went over to one of the back tables and sat down.

Nothing about her life was how she had thought it was. The Craddocks had adopted her. Why hadn't she known? There was nothing in the papers her parents had left to have warned Jenna. Her birth certificate showed Hedra and Tristan as her parents and said that she was born at home. She didn't have to look through them again to know that there had never been a mention of an adoption.

Jenna flashed back to the time when she'd been taken to the orphanage. She had never felt so bewildered or so alone. Jenna realized that the only constant in her life since then was that she had no one…no one at all.

So what was she going to do now? She'd come from Australia on a one-way ticket. She had enough money to live on while she searched for employment. With her references and skills, she expected to have little trouble finding a position.

Morwenna said that the man who had come looking for her had come from Scotland. She considered that information to be a lead of sorts. How strange. A man by the name of Dumas from Edinburgh knew who she was. Was it possible that she had been adopted there? What if the man was her father, trying to find his adult daughter? Maybe he'd moved to America since she was born. If so, that would explain his accent.

Now he was back and was looking for her. Did it matter that she bore no resemblance to him? Perhaps she looked like her mother.

Since meeting Morwenna, Jenna knew she didn't want to stay in Cornwall. There was nothing to stop her from looking for work in Scotland. Perhaps she'd find Mr. Dumas there and he could explain his connection to her.

The thought calmed her. She didn't have much of a lead, but it was something. Someone knew of her existence and had come searching for her. The thought gave her some comfort.

At the moment, it was the only comfort she had.

Chapter Two

"I see that you're Australian, Ms. Craddock. What brings you to Scotland looking for work?"

Jenna sat before a Ms. Violet Spradlin, who ran an employment agency in Edinburgh.

"Actually, I was born in the U.K. and haven't been back in several years. I decided to move to Scotland because I find it breathtakingly beautiful. Since I have no family, I can choose to live wherever I wish, so I chose this region."

"I see." Violet shuffled through several papers before she looked up. "You have an excellent work record according to this recommendation. I'm impressed with your skills for one your age—twenty-five, right? You must have started working quite young."

"Yes."

Violet sighed and said, "Unfortunately, we don't have very much to offer at the moment. It's the nature of the business, you know. I may get several calls in the morning needing someone immediately. One never knows. I hope that you aren't depending on finding a position right away."

"I understand."

Violet peered over her glasses. "How can I contact you if something turns up?"

"I'm staying at a small inn on the outskirts of the city. If you like, I can check in with you every day or so."

Violet glanced at the file and muttered to herself, "Ah, now I see. You put your present lodging down as your address." She looked at Jenna thoughtfully, tapping her pen against the desk. "I don't suppose you'd be interested in a position where room and board is offered, would you?" Before Jenna had a chance to respond, Violet continued. "No, probably not. The position isn't here in Edinburgh and I can't guarantee that you would find your working conditions all that pleasant."

Intrigued by Ms. Spradlin's manner, which seemed to be more discouraging than encouraging, Jenna said, "I wouldn't mind relocating. And being offered lodging as well would make things considerably easier for me, at least, at first."

Violet rose and went to a filing cabinet nearby. She thumbed through several files before saying,

"Ah. I knew it was here somewhere." She pulled out a thick manila file and returned to her desk. She looked at Jenna. "I'm not necessarily recommending this position to you, you understand."

"Yes, I understand." Jenna wondered what the position could be that it warranted such a warning from the woman.

Violet opened the file and began to read. "Sir Ian MacGowan needs a person with good secretarial skills to transcribe his dictation for his novel."

"Oh. An author."

"Well," Violet said slowly, "I suppose you could call him that, although I don't think he's sold anything. He was in an automobile accident a few months ago. Normally he lives in London. However, he decided to return to his family home to rest and recuperate. I believe the process of writing is helping to keep him occupied."

"Oh." Jenna pictured a white-haired gentleman, possibly a little overweight, who wasn't ready to retire quite yet. "You said you don't necessarily recommend this position. I'd like to know why. It sounds like just the position for me. It probably isn't a permanent one, but working for Sir Ian would give me time to get acquainted with the area."

Violet sighed and removed her glasses. She massaged the bridge of her nose as she stared myopically at Jenna. Without saying anything, she carefully cleaned her glasses and replaced them. It was obvious to Jenna that the woman was trying to decide what to say. Was the man some kind of monster? she wondered.

Finally, Violet spoke. "Do you see these papers?" She waved her hand at the open file. "They represent the applicants I have sent Sir Ian during the past several weeks."

"He didn't hire any of them?" Jenna asked. What an odd man.

"After complaining incessantly about the lack of qualifications in the women he interviewed, he finally settled on one who stayed two weeks. The second left after three days." She sighed and shook her head.

"Is he a sexual predator?"

Violet looked startled for a moment before she broke into laughter. "No, no, no. I didn't mean to give you that impression. He's just a very difficult man to work for." She sorted through the papers, reading portions out loud. "'He's short-tempered and impossible to please,' says one. The other says, 'He set impossible time limits on the work I was doing. He's really impossible.'"

"Ah," said Jenna, nodding. "I know just the kind of boss he is." She smiled. "My last employer was that way when I first started to work for him."

Violet's eyebrows rose. "Really. That surprises me. According to his letter of recommendation, he hated to lose you. In fact, if I didn't know better, I would think this was a letter recommending you for sainthood," she said archly.

"He was a very busy man, and until I was hired he hadn't had much luck finding someone who could work with little direction. Once I got past his gruff exterior and convinced him I wasn't a 'lazy twit'—I believe his words were—we managed to work quite well together."

Violet nodded, smiling slightly. "I see. Perhaps you will have more success with Sir Ian than the others."

"When could we set up an interview?"

Violet's brows rose. "Oh, he no longer interviews. He said it takes too much time out of his day. He told me to find someone who wouldn't pester him to death with questions and comments and hire her."

"Sight unseen?"

"If you think you might want the position, of course. Perhaps you might try it and see. If you don't like it you will at least know you tried and perhaps by then something else will have turned up for you. So, what would you like to do?"

Jenna weighed her options. She didn't want to spend any more of her reserves than necessary if she had an opportunity to work. "I would at least like to meet him. Perhaps we'll both agree that I won't suit it, but I dislike turning down the offer without meeting him."

"Good. That's good. If anyone can assist him, my money is on you, Jenna." Violet reached for the phone and dialed a number from the file in front of her. She waited. Jenna could hear the quiet "brrring-brrring" of the phone at the other end. When it was answered, Violet said, "Good morning, Hazel. This is Violet Spradlin at the employment agency. How are you this morning?"

Jenna listened to the one-sided conversation with amusement. They sounded like old friends, which she supposed was possible considering the number of people Violet had sent there. She idly wondered if Hazel was Sir Ian's wife.

"I'd like to speak to Sir Ian," Violet said. "Yes, I know he's busy. Yes. No, I'm not calling about his most recent help. Yes, I know. New employees can be quite trying at times. The reason I'm calling is to let him know that I have hired a secretary for him. I believe she will be just what he's looking for. Yes, that's right. Yes, I'll hold." She looked at Jenna and winked.

After a lengthy wait, Violet said, "Yes, good morn— Yes, I do— As a matter of fact, she's right he—" She covered the phone and asked, "He wants to know when you can come. He seems to be a bit stressed at the moment."

"I could come today if I can get directions how to get there."

"Well, that might work. I did say the position is not here in Edinburgh, didn't I? I would imagine you don't have access to a car."

"No. Will that be a problem?"

Violet spoke into the phone. "She doesn't have

transportation at the moment, Sir Ian. I could have her take the train to Stirling, if you— Oh. Yes. Well, that will work, I'm sure.'' She glanced at Jenna. "She's petite, with reddish blond hair. She's wearing a dark green suit. I don't think she'll be hard to— Yes. I'll tell her.''

Violet hung up the phone. "Well. That was certainly a short discussion. He wants you to take the train to Stirling. He'll have his housekeeper, Hazel Pennington, meet you at the station. Once you've arrived he'll discuss salary and days off with you.''

"All right," Jenna said. Her question about Hazel had been answered. She stood. "I appreciate your willingness to hire me for the position.''

"Don't thank me yet, dear. Wait until you've worked a few weeks with him. Then I'll know you're sincere. Sir Ian is abrupt, but according to Hazel, who's worked for his family for years, he's fair.''

"Have you met him?''

"Not in person, no. But I certainly recognize his voice when I hear it. It's very distinctive.'' Violet touched her throat with her fingers and Jenna could have sworn the older woman actually blushed. Aha. The plot thickens. Maybe Ms. Spradlin has some designs on the old gentleman. Good for her.

Jenna said, "I need to gather my belongings and check out of my room.'' She held out her hand and Violet took it. "Regardless of how this turns out,

I'll still be grateful that you have given me this opportunity.''

"Don't feel that I'm sending you off like a lamb to be slaughtered. I'll be checking with you from time to time. If another position should open up, I'll let you know.''

While Jenna packed the few items she'd unpacked since she'd arrived yesterday afternoon, she thought about what she was doing. She'd accepted a position without meeting her employer first. Given the experience she'd gained working with Basil, she hoped that she could deal with another curmudgeon with little difficulty. She would have to write an amusing letter to Basil and let him know how his training had been put to good use.

Besides, she could visit Edinburgh on her days off and continue her search for Mr. Dumas. As soon as she'd checked in to her room, Jenna had gone through the telephone directory in hopes of finding a listing for him.

There was none.

She'd called the telephone company for any new listings or possibly unlisted numbers. If his number was unlisted, she would at least know he actually lived in Edinburgh or nearby. She'd had no luck there, either. However, she didn't intend to stop looking for the mysterious—at least to her—stranger. She'd hoped to find work in the city, which would make her search easier, but she'd manage.

Once on the train to Stirling, Jenna thought about

her new position. She'd never met an author, published or unpublished. She was curious about what sort of stories he wrote. Perhaps he'd fought in one of the wars and was sharing his experiences. She might find his writing fascinating.

On the other hand, Sir Ian might be a terrible writer. Maybe that was why he was so brusque. Perhaps he was the sort of person who preferred to blame others for his own shortcomings.

What was really important, though, was that she was in Scotland and had a job.

When the train neared the station, Jenna gathered her rather cumbersome bags in preparation for getting off. She had gotten rid of most everything she owned before she came to the U.K. She'd had more than one twinge of regret to see the furniture and furnishings she'd carefully acquired go to strangers. However, the money she received from the sale helped her to feel more secure about her leap into the unknown.

One of the commuters helped with her third bag when she stepped off the train. She thanked him and turned to scan the area. Several people waited to board as others disembarked. Once the train pulled away, Jenna stood alone on the platform.

She had no idea how long a wait she would have for the housekeeper and wished she had a description of her.

Jenna pulled two of the bags behind her, the third

hanging from a strap across her shoulder, and headed toward the depot.

"You must be Jenna Craddock," a cheerful voice said. Jenna paused and looked around. A tall, raw-boned woman of indeterminate age came toward her from the parking lot. "I'm Hazel Pennington, Ian's housekeeper. I apologize for not being here when you arrived. I got behind some slow traffic, which is frustrating enough without needing to be somewhere on time." She took one of the bags and started back toward the stairs.

Jenna hurried to catch up. "How did you know which train to meet? I didn't know which one, myself, until I arrived at the station."

As they loaded the luggage into a utility vehicle, Hazel said, "Oh, Ian knew. He checked the train schedule and chose the one you'd most likely take. If you hadn't been on this one, I would have waited until the next one."

Jenna had many questions about Sir Ian and knew that Hazel would probably be able to answer them. However, she didn't want to appear too anxious about working for him. She sat quietly and listened to the housekeeper as she pointed out various historical sights along the way.

"If you haven't visited Stirling before, you might enjoy touring the William Wallace Monument." Hazel nodded toward a tower in the distance. "The only way up is by stone circular stairs, so you'll want to be in shape for the climb."

When Jenna saw the castle high on an escarpment, she made a sound of awe.

''The castle is worth visiting, as well. There's a military museum there in addition to the carefully restored rooms. There's a cathedral nearby that has become a tourist favorite, as well.''

Jenna's excitement grew as she considered the age of so many historic places in the U.K. compared to the relatively newly settled Australia.

She eagerly tried to see everything they passed on their way north. The scenery was breathtaking. She could hardly wait to begin exploring. She would continue to look for a listing for Mr. Dumas wherever she went. Surely, she would find him sometime.

Hazel turned into a driveway no more than half an hour's drive from Stirling, catching Jenna off guard. From the way Ms. Spradlin talked, Jenna had expected to find an isolated home deep in the countryside.

They followed a narrow lane, and from the way it nestled into the earth, it no doubt had been in existence for centuries. Massive trees marched along on each side, their bare branches arching over like a canopy. Jenna could only imagine their beauty in the summer, covered with green foliage.

She noticed a large and, no doubt, ancient wall that followed beside the lane. If only those stones could talk, she thought. They must have witnessed a great deal of history.

The lane made a sharp turn at the end and Hazel

drove through an arched opening. Jenna saw a paved parking area in front of an honest-to-goodness castle. This is where Sir Ian lived?

"This is absolutely wonderful," Jenna said reverently, looking around her. "I can't imagine what it must be like to have grown up in such a place. It would be like living in an enchanted castle."

Hazel opened the back of the utility vehicle without glancing around. "It's an ancient piece of rubbish, is what it is, but we're all quite fond of it. It takes a fortune to maintain, of course. There's always something to repair. If it isn't the vintage wiring, we're sure to find a leaky pipe somewhere." She pulled Jenna's luggage out and set it on the ground.

Jenna grabbed the handle of the heaviest one and leaned to place the one with the shoulder strap over her shoulder. Hazel stopped her. "I can get these two," she said, matching her actions to her words. She carried the bags as though they were empty.

Jenna followed her to the entrance. Two beautifully carved doors were set in an arch similar to the one they had driven through. Jenna gazed at the massive example of skilled craftsmanship in awe. Once they entered, Hazel set the luggage into a recessed area near the door and said, "We'll leave these here for now. Ian is eager to speak with you. Let's not keep him waiting. Afterward I can show you where you'll be staying."

Jenna looked up and blinked. The lofty ceiling of

the great hall soared at least thirty feet. Family crests and giant oil paintings of people from earlier times covered the wide expanse. Immediately beneath the ceiling, fan-shaped windows filled both ends of the four-walled entrance room.

Hazel paused in front of a closed door near the wide staircase that curved to the second floor. Jenna could almost see the graceful women who had lived here sweep down the stairs in their beautiful gowns.

The vision abruptly disappeared when Hazel opened the door and said, "Ms. Craddock is here."

"Good," a rumbling voice said. "Send her in."

Chapter Three

Jenna caught herself holding her breath. She consciously took another deep breath, exhaled and stepped into the room. Once inside she discovered a book-lined library that would cause an avid reader—which she was—to mentally salivate with anticipation. She almost chuckled at the idea of living in a castle with access to such a treasure trove of riches. The idea sounded too good to be true.

She took in everything in the few seconds before she looked at the man standing in front of the fireplace. Once she focused on Ian MacGowan, the room faded into the background. The commanding energy emanating from him inexorably drew her eye.

She immediately revised her mental picture of a white-haired elderly curmudgeon. Sir Ian bore no resemblance to such a person. For one thing, he was far from old—somewhere in his early to mid-thirties, she guessed. Instead of white hair, his was light brown. It curled riotously over his forehead and around his ears like a young child's—and looked so soft and silky, her palms itched to touch it.

She had a sudden vision of a laird standing there, the family crest mounted above the mantel. Golden brown eyes beneath thick brows scrutinized her. A noticeable cleft in his chin drew her eye, and she thought he would be quite attractive if it weren't for the frown that seemed etched into his face.

He held a cane in his left hand and she noticed that his weight rested on his right leg. A scar ran along his temple and a smaller one bisected his left brow. There were signs of suffering in his face.

"Come," he said, motioning his hand impatiently. "I won't bite you, for God's sake. Stop hovering at the door." He motioned to one of the chairs arranged in front of a brisk fire. "Sit."

Now that he had spoken, Jenna could better understand Ms. Spradlin's reaction to him. His deep voice sent a shiver of sensual awareness through her even while his manner of speaking irritated her. If she was going to be working for him, she needed to set some ground rules.

"Yes, I will, thank you," she replied graciously, crossing the room. "As you know, I'm Jenna Craddock and I've come to transcribe your work for you.

However, I would appreciate your not using dog commands when speaking to me. I'm perfectly capable of responding to entire sentences.'' She held out her hand to him.

He looked at her hand in surprise before he briefly shook it. ''Ian MacGowan,'' he muttered brusquely, his frown deepening. With exaggerated politeness, he said, ''Please have a seat, if you would be so kind.''

No eye-rolling, she reminded herself. If she intended to work for the man she would need to adjust to his sarcasm and abrupt manner.

Once she was seated, Sir Ian limped to a nearby chair and carefully lowered himself, his jaw flexing when he bent his left knee. She made a point to focus on his face, most especially his eyes. When he made eye contact she smiled at him, folded her hands and waited for him to speak.

Abruptly, he said, ''You're not what I expected.''

Her smile widened. ''You come as a bit of a shock, as well,'' she said, intending to voice her thought that he would be older. ''Mrs. Spradlin didn't mention—'' That was as far as she got when he interrupted her.

''I'm sure my reputation precedes me,'' he said irritably. ''That ninny Spradlin must lead a very boring life to get so much titillation out of my search for a decent secretary.''

Oh, my. Sir Ian was definitely an irascible sort. ''She mentioned that you've been without an assistant for a few weeks.

"Through no fault of my own, I assure you. The woman has an absolute knack for sending me the most inept or overly sensitive women who fall apart whenever I frown at them, raise my voice or point out a typing error. The last one left in tears, the silly thing. You're from Australia."

Jenna blinked at the sudden change of subject. "Yes, Sir Ian, I am."

He rolled his eyes. "Forget the title and call me Ian." He pulled at his earlobe. "I've asked Ms. Spradlin more than once not to use my title but she's too busy chattering on to hear me."

From her observation during the conversation in Ms. Spradlin's office, she knew he had been busy interrupting while Ms. Spradlin was speaking.

"I would think being a knight is a great honor," she said lightly.

"You would, would you? Tell me something about yourself," he said abruptly. "You're young— I can see that. Are you single?"

One brow lifted. "Yes."

"I don't want you to think you can move someone else in with you—married or single."

That comment didn't merit an answer.

"Why did you leave Australia?"

She held his gaze and smiled deliberately. "To see the world."

"Why Scotland?"

"Why not? I like it here."

He leaned back in his chair, staring at her from beneath his frowning brows. He had to be aware of how intimidating he looked. She wondered if he used that look to keep his employees in their proper place. She almost smiled at the thought. He might be laird of his castle but he would quickly discover that she wasn't easily intimidated.

What did it matter to him why she was there? she wondered. Perhaps he enjoyed irritating people.

After a rather lengthy silence while he stared at her, he said, "Okay, now I get it. This is a joke, isn't it? Todd told you to show up here, didn't he?" He spoke in short, abrupt spurts. And his mind seemed to jump around like a grasshopper. She wondered if he was on pain medication. Being on drugs might explain his lack of focus and, to her at least, his strange remarks.

"Todd?" she repeated.

"Yes, Todd, my supervisor. He probably got tired of hearing me complain about not being able to find decent help and sent you to help out. Not that I'm bothered by the ruse, you understand. I need someone competent and Todd would make certain of that, at least. But there's no reason for you to hide the fact."

"Since I've no idea what you do for a living—other than write, that is—I have no idea who your supervisor might be. Why would you think I would lie about my reasons for being here? Are you always so suspicious of people?"

"Yes."

Great. Paranoid, as well. He was going to be a joy to work with, she could see that already.

"Your story doesn't quite work," he said gruffly. "There's no reason that I can see for you to come to Scotland in the first place, much less apply for work. If you're serious about living in the U.K., London would be the most logical place for you to search for work."

Was this some kind of test? Was she supposed to break down in tears at this point? Calmly Jenna replied, "Do you have a particular reason for questioning my honesty, sir? You may not believe me but I have no reason to lie to you." She stood and ran her hands down her thighs to smooth her skirt. "You've made it quite clear that once again you're displeased with Ms. Spradlin's choice. I respect that. You certainly have the right to disagree with her." She picked up her handbag. "I do want to reassure you, however, that I didn't accept the position with some nefarious plan in mind. I merely wanted a job. Your family's heirlooms would have been safe with me."

Jenna walked toward the door, mentally telling the rows of books goodbye.

"Oh, for God's sake, stop being so melodramatic," Ian snapped. "Come back here. I don't want to be hopping up and down every time I say something that displeases you."

She turned and looked at him. "It isn't melodramatic to dislike rudeness, sir. I'm capable of dealing with a great many foibles, but I will not tolerate your disrespect."

He pushed himself out of his chair and faced her.

Their gazes locked and she, for one, did not intend to back down. She felt a small victory of sorts when he glanced away and muttered something that might have been an apology.

Or a curse word.

"Let's start over, shall we?" he asked, running his hand through his hair. Definitely irritated, she thought to herself. Well, so was she. "Please sit." When she was seated once again, he said, "May I see your references?"

Without replying, Jenna reached into her purse and brought out her résumé and two letters of recommendation. After handing them to him, she waited for his next salvo.

After reading the documents, he looked at her and said, "According to this, your previous employer is convinced you walk on water. With this glowing recommendation, I'm surprised he allowed you to leave." He studied her for a moment. "Did your departure have anything to do with a lover's spat? Because if it did, I see no reason to have you settle in here only to receive an apologetic phone call from him that will send you scurrying back to Australia…with all due respect."

"Not that such information is any of your business, but since Basil Fitzgerald is sixty-five years old with several children and grandchildren, I doubt he could have found time for an affair…and if he had ever entertained the idea, Mrs. Fitzgerald would have bashed him on the head for considering it."

"If I seem to be prying into your personal life,

Ms. Craddock, I do apologize. I need an assistant who will focus on my work. What you do on your own time is up to you. Just so we're clear about our arrangement, I'm not looking for a personal relationship with you. I don't have time for flirting or any of that nonsense. I need a skilled assistant. That's all.''

Jenna fought to hang on to her temper. Fighting for control, she studied the man, allowing her gaze to slide over him from his curls to his rather large feet. Eventually she raised her eyes to meet his and said, "Tell me, *Sir* Ian, are you always this obnoxious or did I luck out and catch you on a bad day? I can't for the life of me imagine why you think that I—or any other self-respecting woman, for that matter—would be interested in having a relationship with you.''

He looked startled for a moment, then gave her a boyish grin that was wholly unexpected...and devastatingly attractive. "You'll do, Ms. Craddock. You'll do.'' Before she could find her voice to tell him that she wasn't at all certain she wished to work for him, Ian mentioned a salary that made her eyes widen. The sum was at least twice what she'd expected to receive, taking into account that her room and board were part of the compensation. For that amount of money, she'd be willing to work for Attila the Hun. From what she had gathered so far, the man could very well be the reincarnation of Attila.

"I hope you'll find your stay here satisfactory,''

he said. He stood, wincing as he straightened his left leg. "I'll have Hazel show you to your room."

He touched a button on the extension phone next to his chair and Jenna heard Hazel's voice. "Yes?"

"I believe Ms. Craddock and I have dealt with the necessary hiring procedures. Will you show her to her room, please?"

"Certainly."

Jenna rose and walked to the door. When she opened it, she saw Hazel striding down the hallway toward her. As Jenna stepped through the doorway, Ian spoke again. "Ms. Craddock?"

She turned. "Yes?"

"Do I have your permission to call you Jenna?"

She doubted the sincerity of his conciliatory tone. With a regal nod, she answered, "Yes."

His lips twitched. "Well, then, welcome aboard, Jenna. I would appreciate your returning as soon as you've settled in. I hope you won't feel too rushed to begin working today. As you're aware, I've been without help for some time."

She lifted one brow and said, "Imagine that," before quietly closing the door behind her.

Chapter Four

Ian drummed his fingers on the arm of his chair and stared into the fire as he waited for Jenna Craddock.

He'd never met anyone like her and he hadn't expected her to be so young.

When he'd spoken to Violet Spradlin many weeks ago, he'd made it clear that he wanted a competent, no-nonsense assistant. He'd pictured a middle-aged woman who did what she was hired to do. Someone dependable…like Hazel. Most of the women he'd interviewed fit that description.

The last thing he'd expected was a petite woman with sparkling eyes and a charming smile. Not that she'd been smiling by the time their meeting was over, he reminded himself. She might as well learn that he didn't have time for social chitchat. He had a busy schedule, what with his physical therapy three times a week, the exercises he needed to do to get back in top form and working on his novel.

He'd been grateful to have something besides pain to occupy his mind these past months. Who would have believed that he would find enjoyment doing something so out of his professional field? But he'd always been an avid reader. He wasn't certain when he first thought about writing a book—probably during one of the nights when pain kept him awake. Whatever the reason for beginning the project, he was hooked.

He'd had no idea what he was doing when he started out, but somehow he began to realize what he wanted to say. He would revise, and revise again, until the story read more like the one he could hear in his head.

Life was full of surprises.

Jenna Craddock was one of them.

Her looks should be irrelevant but he'd turned into something of a hermit since the accident. His only visitor was Hal, his physical therapist, who irritated him to no end, always harping about not overdoing it.

He would do whatever was necessary to get back to top form. He'd devoted twelve years of his life to his job, and he wouldn't allow his injuries to put an end to his career.

That career didn't leave him time to develop a

relationship with a woman. Therefore, he'd never been seriously involved with anyone. One woman went so far as to point out that he was married to his career, "whatever it was." All she knew was that two to three months would pass without word from him. There were very few women willing to see him on his schedule.

His mother had already despaired of becoming a grandmother, he thought, amused. Not that she ever gave up haranguing him about the notion. He'd tried to convince her that he couldn't find another woman like her, but she would have none of it.

Now he was faced with a situation where he'd become unavoidably celibate. The last thing he needed was a nubile young woman around him on a daily basis as a constant reminder of what he was missing.

He would work around the problem, that's all. He'd make certain to maintain a professional relationship with her. Since he took most of his meals in his room anyway, he doubted he'd see her when she wasn't working.

The important thing was to finish the novel. Once it was done, she would be leaving. Another spur to finish the novel as rapidly as possible. If by some fluke he actually sold the thing—and what a long chance that was—he intended to use the money for needed repairs to his home.

In his case his home really was a castle—a money-gobbling anachronism. He preferred his flat in London. As his parents were wont to remind him, though, his home was a monument to the past and was his legacy as a MacGowan.

Lucky him.

The Security Service continued to pay him his full salary, which he appreciated.

Ian glanced at his watch. He hoped Jenna would stay until the book was finished. Afterward, he would no longer need her…or anyone else.

Jenna followed Hazel as they turned down yet another hallway from the top of the stairs.

The stairs continued to the next floor. She'd seen photographs of five-star hotels no larger than this place. Antique weapons and paintings of men in kilts and women wrapped in the bold plaid of the MacGowans decorated the walls.

Sconces provided light in the dim hallways, and Jenna almost laughed out loud at the sudden image of being locked away in a Gothic castle with a beast. Her active imagination had helped her survive the uncertainties of her childhood and it continued to flourish. She reminded herself that, since she was no beauty, she doubted she would be living out that particular fairy tale.

"This place is huge," she murmured.

"I know," Hazel replied, "but you'll get used to it. All but this wing are closed, which is a shame, really, with so much history on display. The historical society has asked more than once for permission to bring tours through the unused parts of the castle. I've pointed out to Ian that the added income would help to keep up with the maintenance. But he tells them no. He says he doesn't want to stumble over strangers in his own home.''

"It must take an army to keep up with the cleaning.''

Hazel chuckled. "As a matter of fact, it does. Periodically we have several of the women in the village come in and do the heavy cleaning. Two of them come in on a weekly basis to clean this section.''

"I feel fortunate to be able to live here.''

"Oh, it would be too much to ask you to commute from one of the villages when we have all this room. I'm pleased that you seem to appreciate it.'' She paused in front of one of the doors. "Personally, I'm glad to have the company. Before Ian returned home, Cook and I rattled around the place except on cleaning days. Ian doesn't entertain and rarely has overnight visitors. He prefers his own company, you see.''

"Yes, I did get that impression," she replied wryly as Hazel opened the door.

"Oh, dear. I hope he didn't put you off from working for him. He's a dear, really. Just a trifle impatient. He's eager to return to work.''

"I see," Jenna replied politely if not truthfully. He hadn't mentioned his profession to her. Since she was there to transcribe his novel, whatever else he did was none of her business.

Hazel walked into the room and said, "Here we are. I hope you'll be comfortable." She crossed the sitting room and opened a door. "Your bedroom is through here. It has an attached bath. During the latest remodeling, the MacGowans decided to turn the bedrooms into comfortable apartments with modern conveniences, including some much-needed closet space."

Jenna was speechless. She'd had no idea that she would be living in what looked to be a royal apartment, with its ornate woodwork and cornices, rich draperies and rugs, as well as museum-quality furniture.

"I'm trying not to think of my being here as part of a fairy tale, but it's difficult not to with everything you've shown me."

"Complete with an ogre when Ian's in one of his moods."

Jenna burst into surprised laughter. "I was thinking along the same lines. Oh, my, it isn't at all polite to joke about my employer." She could feel her cheeks glow with embarrassment.

"Don't worry about it. Ian has a great sense of humor. He just keeps it packed away most of the time until it must get rusty with disuse." Hazel walked back into the sitting room. "If there's anything you need, please let me know."

Jenna smiled. "Thank you. This is wonderful. I

feel as though I should be paying you for the privilege of living here.''

''Don't worry. After a few days of working to catch up with Ian, you'll feel that you've more than earned your keep!'' With a quick wave of her hand, Hazel left the room.

Jenna knew she needed to return downstairs as soon as possible, but after Hazel left she couldn't resist taking a peek out the windows. When she did she discovered that she had a bird's-eye view of extensive gardens that were obviously planned to be a showcase.

She promised herself a closer look as soon as possible, but for now she needed to freshen up and return to where Ian awaited her. She didn't need to incur his displeasure by dawdling.

Once in the hallway, she looked around her, hoping to gain some familiarity with her section of the castle. Too bad she hadn't thought to sprinkle bread crumbs on the way to her quarters so she could find her way back to the library. Shades of some gothic novel where a castle holds myriad secrets for an unsuspecting employee to discover!

Luckily she found her way with only one detour. Ian stepped out of the library as she came down the last few steps. With a short nod by way of acknowledging her presence, Ian said, ''I'll show you to your office.''

This close to him, Jenna was acutely aware of his size. She barely came to his shoulder. There must be Viking blood in his veins. She could picture one of his ancestors wielding a five-foot sword during a clan dispute without breaking a sweat.

"Here we are," he said, and opened a door at the back of the hallway. He motioned for her to enter. When she did, she was pleasantly surprised to see that the room was quite cozy and well lit from a bank of windows. She would enjoy working here.

"This is quite lovely," she said, smiling. A computer sat at a fully equipped workstation.

"I believe you'll find everything you need."

She followed him to the desk and quickly scanned its contents. She nodded without looking at him.

He pointed to a stack of tapes. "These are the tapes I mentioned. They must look overwhelming to you and for that, I'm sorry. Do the best you can." He glanced at her and added, "Do you think you'll be able to manage?"

"Don't worry. I really am well trained for this sort of thing."

"Good. After you print out what you've transcribed, leave it on my desk in the library. If you have questions and I'm not available, attach a note to the place and I'll answer it when I can. Any questions?"

"No. I believe you've been quite clear."

"You haven't asked about days off."

Amused, she said, "Not with that much work waiting for me. I don't dare," she said, grinning. "Don't worry. I'll let you know when I need a break. I'm fairly flexible about working out a routine. If I fear that you're taking advantage of my good nature," she added, tongue in cheek, "I will—of course—immediately make it known to you."

He gave an abrupt nod and turned away. Without looking back he said, "I'll leave it to you, then."

Once the door closed behind him, Jenna pulled out the chair and sat in front of the computer. She turned it on and was pleased to see that the latest in software programs had been installed. She picked up the first tape, placed it in the transcribing machine, adjusted the earphones and began her new job, four hours after leaving her interview with Violet Spradlin.

While Ian went through his physical therapy program that afternoon, he recalled the incident that had almost killed him. It had been the basis of many a nightmare during the past few months.

As a member of the Security Service, the U.K.'s civilian intelligence agency, he was used to covert operations. Only a handful of people knew what he actually did for the government. Even his parents thought he had a desk job somewhere in the maze of government offices.

His last assignment called for him to infiltrate a terrorist cell. In the midst of a meeting that took place in the basement of an abandoned building, one of their explosives went off without warning.

Several were killed outright. He would have been,

as well, if he hadn't been somewhat protected by a concrete pillar.

The blast had thrown him several feet. When he landed, his left arm and leg were broken and his knee was damaged.

He didn't remember anything about the explosion. The first he knew something had happened was when he became fully conscious in the hospital.

The pain had pulled him out of the gentle darkness where he rested. The throbbing rhythm had coursed through him, which had told him he'd been hurt badly.

"Ian," a quiet voice said, "wake up. We need to talk."

His supervisor, Todd Brewster, stood beside the bed watching him when Ian forced his eyes open.

"Did you get the license number of the lorry that ran over me?" Ian said hoarsely.

"I asked them to ease up on the pain medication long enough for you to be able to talk."

"How thoughtful of you," Ian muttered. "What happened?"

"What do you remember?"

Ian forced himself to concentrate, his sluggish brain slow to respond. "The last thing I remember was the cell meeting."

"Do you recall what was discussed?"

Ian did his best to report details. He ended with "Who else was hurt?"

"Out of the five there, three were killed outright

and the other is in critical condition. We decided that the identity you assumed was also killed.''

Ian closed his eyes. After a moment Todd said, ''The word is that you were in a bad car smash-up. You'll be on medical leave with full pay until you recover.''

''Since I'm wearing casts on my arm and leg, I presume they're broken. What else?''

''Your leg is broken in two places. Your shoulder was dislocated and your wrist broken. However, it's your knee that has the surgeons most concerned. It'll be a while before you have full use of it.''

''Just what I needed.''

''My suggestion is for you to go home—not your flat—to Scotland. Come back when you're better.''

''What if my knee doesn't improve? What then?''

''Let's don't do worst-case scenarios right now. You're damn lucky to be alive. Once the doctors release you I'll have one of our people drive you to Scotland.''

Ian had nodded and had watched as Todd had left the room. There'd been a great deal left unsaid. The most important had been whether or not he would work again.

''That's enough for the day, Ian.'' He was brought back to the present when Hal, his trainer, said, ''I'm amazed at the progress you've made since I've been coming here. I didn't think your knee would ever become as flexible as it has. You never acknowledge the pain. It's only when you turn white that I know you're pushing yourself past your limits.''

''The pain doesn't matter. What matters is that my leg becomes fully functional.''

After he showered and dressed, Ian went to check on Jenna. He found her typing so fast her fingers were a blur. He waited until she paused before speaking. ''Are the tapes decipherable?''

She started and removed her earphones. ''Sorry. I didn't know you were there.'' She paused, as though searching for words. ''The tape fades in and out at times. It could be the recorder.''

''Or my dictation. I pace while I talk. I'll watch how I hold the mike in the future.''

''I was wondering if I could run out a copy of what's already been transcribed before today. I'd like to be able to understand the story.''

''Whatever helps you.''

''This is a spy thriller, isn't it?''

''Of sorts, I suppose.''

''Where did you get the idea for your novel?''

''I'm writing what I like to read.''

She smiled. ''Oh, I thought you might be writing from experience.''

He lifted his brow. ''Hardly.''

''Ah. Well, then, you have a very lively imagination.''

''Sorry to have disturbed you. I'll let you get back

to work.'' He turned and walked to the door, the sound of the soft clicking of the keyboard accompanying him.

Jenna felt she had made some progress by the time she went up to her room that night. Before going to sleep, she read the first seventy-five pages of Ian's novel. By the time she'd caught up with the story, Jenna was hooked.

The book was definitely about espionage, as she'd surmised. His protagonist, a government agent, was in hot water by page five.

She wondered what Ian's job was. Perhaps he was an accountant fantasizing about living life dangerously.

She went to sleep smiling at the thought.

Jenna had been there for several days when she awoke early to discover that the ever-constant clouds and damp weather that seemed to be a permanent condition in Scotland had been chased away by the glorious sun. Light poured into her windows, gilding everything.

Too excited to sleep, she hurriedly dressed for the day. She must have been too distracted to notice where she was going because somehow she managed to miss a turn and found herself wandering through dimly lit hallways in an effort to find her way downstairs.

''That's what you get for not paying attention,'' she muttered to herself. ''You'll lose the extra time before work trying to find your way out of the place.'' She felt like some heroine in a novel, lost in the endless halls of an ancient castle. All she needed was an armored suit to come to life and start clanking its way toward her and she'd be screaming.

She came across a gallery lined with oil paintings—no doubt a pictorial display of the Mac-Gowans down through history. She wished she had time to study them and promised herself that she would come back sometime soon—if she ever managed to find the place again.

Jenna gave an audible sigh of relief when she spotted some narrow stairs leading downward. She hurried down them and opened the door at the bottom of the stairwell. She couldn't say who was the most startled when she found herself in the kitchen—she or the woman working at the counter.

''Oops,'' she said, laughing. ''Sorry to bother you. I'm Jenna Craddock, Sir Ian's secretary. If you could point me toward the dining room I'll get out of your way.''

The woman chuckled. ''Certainly,'' she said. ''I'm Megan MacKinnock, better known as Cook. Follow me.''

The smell of fresh coffee greeted Jenna when she stepped into the dining room from the kitchen. She took her meals in an alcove surrounded by windows. Every time she had occasion to enter the dining room—which was usually for breakfast only—she felt as though she should be wearing clothes from a hundred years ago. The room and its massive table could easily seat a hundred people with no difficulty. It was a shame that it was so seldom used. She had a sudden flash of another century where genteel women and courtly gentlemen filled the room while candlelight was reflected in all the mirrors.

Mustn't fall into one of your romantic daydreams, she reminded herself. Since coming here, she'd helped herself to several books in Ian's library. She had always enjoyed history as a child, whether in textbooks or in historical novels. She found English and Scottish history most appealing. She would envision herself fighting at Bannockburn and later at Culloden, wielding her sword in a mighty rush to save her people.

Sometimes she wondered if her ancestors might be Scottish. If they were, it would be a little eerie to think that she'd always been on the side of Scotland long before she'd discovered that she was Scottish.

"Good morning, Jenna," Hazel said as she came through the door. "Did you sleep well?"

"Quite well, thank you."

"Cook said you got lost this morning."

"Just a case of not paying enough attention to where I was going."

"Have you seen Ian this morning?" Hazel asked.

"No, but that isn't surprising. I've yet to see him at mealtimes."

"Don't take it personally. He's always been taciturn, even as a boy. I used to tease him about being the typical dour Scotsman.''

''It's difficult for me to imagine Ian as a young boy,'' Jenna admitted.

From directly behind her, he said, ''It wasn't a pretty sight, I grant you,'' which caused Jenna to jump. To Hazel he said, ''See what you can do about getting Hamish out here tomorrow. The leak in my shower has gotten worse.''

''I'll see what I can do, but you know Hamish. He prefers fishing to working.''

''Do what you can.'' He turned and started for the door.

''Aren't you going to eat?'' Hazel asked.

''Not now. Later, maybe.''

Jenna was embarrassed that Ian had found her chatting about him with Hazel. She helped herself to some fruit and a muffin from the array of food on the sideboard, poured herself some coffee and with anticipation gazed out the window at the gardens.

Ian had reached the library before he realized that Hazel had followed him. He stopped and looked at her. ''What?'' he growled impatiently.

''You were rude to Jenna this morning, ignoring her as though she wasn't there. I was wondering, how are things between you and Jenna?''

''What are you talking about? There's nothing between Jenna and me!''

Hazel smiled. "I meant, how is she getting along with your work?"

"Oh. Well, she's very efficient. Impressive, actually. The woman actually knows how to spell as well as punctuate. Will wonders never cease?"

"I thought she looked quite nice this morning, didn't you?"

"I didn't notice." He expected lightning to strike him at any moment. "Is there some point to this interrogation? If not, I have work to do."

"I won't keep you, then," Hazel replied and walked away, a slight smile on her face.

What was all that about? He was doing his best not to think about Jenna. The last thing he needed was to have someone point out her positive attributes to him!

Her laugh seemed to echo through the place as she talked to Hazel. He sometimes wondered when she had time to get any work done. He couldn't complain there, though. Whenever he went into her office for any reason, she was always working. He'd formed a bad habit of going to her office on a daily basis, ostensibly to check on her progress. He was kidding himself, he knew. He'd discovered that he couldn't stay away from her.

When he'd seen her earlier standing there bathed in the sunlight pouring through the dining room window, his heart had missed a beat. She looked like a sprite, aglow with joy and life.

What was the matter with him, waxing poetic

over an employee? Stifling his irritation with him-self, Ian strode into the library to find a reference book he needed.

Jenna hurried outside after hastily swallowing half of her second cup of coffee. As soon as she stepped into the sunshine she stopped and closed her eyes.

Was it her imagination, or was it warmer this morning? She wondered if spring would ever arrive in Scotland. She'd come from summer in Australia without giving much thought to the differences in the climates between the two places. She opened her eyes and took in a lungful of fresh air. The scene was so peaceful that it moved her soul.

With such a beautiful layout of flower beds, she could hardly wait to see the pathways and the foun-tains surrounded by blooms. She followed a crushed-shell path, stopping to study the different plants and shrubs, hoping to discover what they were.

A path crossed the one she was on and on impulse she followed it. Each turn of the path led her to more shrubs and topiaries that fascinated her.

Eventually she glanced at her watch and, with a sigh, turned back toward the castle. There was no getting lost out here. The looming edifice towered over the area. Since the library entrance was closest to her office, Jenna entered the French doors before she discovered Ian standing there watching her.

"Hello, again," she said pleasantly. "Isn't it a beautiful morning?"

He glanced outside as though noticing the weather for the first time. "I suppose. You like the gardens, I see."

"Yes. They're truly beautiful. They must be spectacular when they're in bloom."

"I'm pleased you enjoy them." He turned away. "I hope you found breakfast satisfactory," he said, suddenly taking an inordinate interest in a row of books.

She was dying here. His politeness was so stilted she wanted to laugh, but didn't dare. "Quite satisfactory. If you'll excuse me, I need to get dressed for work."

He turned and looked at her. "What's wrong with the way you're dressed now? There's no dress code, you know." He sounded irritated.

"True," she replied peaceably.

"I, uh, left a couple of tapes on your desk that may need some explanation. I'll be in shortly to discuss them with you."

She noticed a large stack of mail and papers on his desk. It would take him a while to plow through all of that. She nodded and left the room.

Jenna dearly wished her heart wouldn't start pounding every time she saw the man. She was being ridiculous. It wasn't fear. So why did her pulse rate jump each time she saw him? There was just something about him. He seemed so...so...masculine, for lack of a better word.

The tapes were there as well as a large stack of typed pages he'd revised. She'd left them for him the evening before. "Don't you ever sleep?" she murmured to herself.

"Not much," he replied from directly behind her.

She must have jumped six inches off the floor at the sound of his voice. She turned and frowned at him. "I do wish you wouldn't sneak up on a person like that," she said, her hand on her heart.

"I made no effort to be quiet. Are you always this jumpy?"

"Not usually, no."

"Do I make you nervous?"

She didn't want to go there, so she asked, "You wanted to discuss something with me?"

"Yes. I decided to speak with you before I deal with other matters." He paused, and then said, "And I wish you'd sit so that I can. My leg is being particularly uncooperative this morning."

"Oh. Sorry."

She perched on the chair in front of the computer while he pulled an armless chair around to face her. Once seated, he said, "I know I'm not very good at giving you feedback on the work you're doing. I wanted to say that I'm quite impressed with your work. You've been a considerable help and I wanted to thank you."

"Oh."

"I also think this would be a good time to discuss your time off."

"All right."

"Rather than setting a particular schedule, what I suggest is that you take an afternoon off whenever you've caught up with me. It's become obvious that I don't have to worry about your getting behind. In addition, Sundays will be your regular day off. If you wish to take a weekend off, we can discuss scheduling that, as well."

"Thank you."

"I've especially appreciated the questions and suggestions about the characters and plot that you've inserted in the margins. Your insights have been very valuable to me. Well, I—uh—I seem to have hit a glitch in my story. I was wondering if I could discuss what I see as a problem with you. If you prefer not to become that involved, I can respect that, of course."

Surprised and—she admitted to herself—flattered, Jenna replied, "I would enjoy that very much."

For the next hour Ian explained to her why he was concerned. "Philip isn't coming alive as I hoped. I wondered if you might have some suggestions on how I might change that."

Jenna wasn't certain what to say. She'd noticed that the main character was rather two-dimensional. She'd put that down to Ian's probable lack of knowledge of the world about which he was writing.

He must have sensed her hesitation, because he

said, 'Don't worry about hurting my feelings. I need an objective opinion.''

"Well, I suppose the problem may lie in the fact that you never discuss his feelings. You tell us what he does, how he does it, why he gets into such tough situations. What you don't tell us is how he feels about what's going on.''

Ian looked startled, then frowned. "What does that have to do with anything? He's doing his job. It's what he's paid to do. Why describe his emotions?''

"Because that will help readers to relate to him. You tell us what he's thinking, which is good. We also need to know what he's feeling.''

After waiting a few moments, she added, "That's just my opinion, of course. It's your book, after all.''

He waved his hand as though brushing her words away. "What if he doesn't think about what he's feeling? He doesn't have time.''

"True, particularly in the action scenes. I understand that. However, I think it would enrich the narrative if there were also scenes of reflection—when he has to face what has happened and how he feels about it.''

His perpetual frown intensified, which was something of a feat in itself.

"I believe that you need to get into his head— hear his thoughts, feel his reactions.'' She watched him struggle with the idea. In a gentle voice, she said, "From everything I've heard and read about writing, it's suggested that a new writer write about what he knows. Intelligence agents make great protagonists. However, for your first novel, it might have been better to choose an easier subject to write about.''

All expression was wiped off his face at her words and Jenna knew she had overstepped her boundaries. ''Don't mind me,'' she hastily added. ''Not being a writer myself, I have no idea what kind of struggle you must have had to come up with a plot that would catch readers' attention. You've certainly managed to do that.''

He stood and said, ''Perhaps I should have chosen a different subject. I'll see what I can do to dream up a few emotions an agent might have.''

She watched him leave the room, his limp more noticeable than usual. She'd hurt his feelings and she felt badly about pointing out what she thought the protagonist needed to become believable.

Next time she would make certain she didn't respond quite so candidly.

Chapter Five

Jenna was jolted out of her concentration one May morning when Ian stepped into her line of sight. She immediately pulled her earphones away, hoping he hadn't noticed her start of surprise. He had gotten into the habit of wandering in to talk about the book. She was pleased that he used her as a sounding board.

"Good morning," she said, smiling.

He frowned.

"Did you sleep well?" she asked.

"Not particularly. No."

She'd become used to his various moods and had grown tolerant of them, although it would help if someone would post warnings each day. Grumpy, with a growl or two. Lost in his thoughts, won't remember seeing you. Irritated with something that wasn't working, either in the novel or at the castle. She wondered if he had a relaxed mood…or, hard to believe, a happy mood. Despite her vivid imagination, she couldn't visualize that one.

He rubbed his leg, a sign that he was having trouble with it this morning. She asked quietly, "Are you in pain?"

He looked at her distractedly at first before he focused on her. "What are you talking about?"

"The fact that you were massaging your leg together with the agonized look on your face."

"I was thinking."

- She hid her smile. "Ah."

Impatiently he said, "I came to ask you something, but I've forgotten what it was."

She grinned. "Don't you hate when that happens?"

"Uh. Yes, actually I do. The next scene popped into my head after I left my room. Now I'm mentally retracing my steps, trying to recall what prompted me to come looking for you."

She didn't want to interrupt his journey back in time, so she waited.

"Yes, that's it," he muttered. "I wanted to find out what you thought about the revisions I made."

She didn't recall seeing recent revisions. "Which ones?" She hastily thumbed through a stack of marked-up papers.

"The ones explaining his, uh, his feelings."

Oh. He'd done those last week and she hadn't thought to offer her comments. "Oh, those revisions. They were great. You've rounded out his character quite nicely. He seems very real to me...tough when he has to be, but carrying the scars of what he's been forced to do."

He frowned. "You saw that in the book?"

"Well, yes. Wasn't I supposed to?"

He gave his head a shake. "It doesn't matter."

"I'm also amazed by the amount of detail you've included throughout the book. Your story seems very authentic."

"You think so?"

"Absolutely. Your novel is definitely going to be a page-turner."

"Good. That's good, I guess."

"As long as we're discussing what I like about the story, I want to add that I'm also impressed with your secondary characters. If I didn't know this is fiction, I would think they're real people."

His lips twitched and there was almost a smile on his face. Without the perpetual frown, the man was quite attractive.

On impulse, Jenna asked, "Ian, what do you do for fun?"

He looked at her as though she had spoken in a foreign language.

"I beg your pardon?"

"You know, what do you do to relax, to have fun…such as hobbies, sports and such?"

"I never had time for hobbies before the accident. I read, of course, and I write. Those are my hobbies at the moment."

"You really need to get out more. Socialize. Take a break from the book. Do you realize that you haven't had any company since I've been here?"

"I prefer being alone for now. Writing and exercising take all my energy. I'll get out in the world once I return to work."

This was a chance to casually ask what he did for a living. Since he'd never volunteered the information she was hesitant to pry. During the whole time she had been transcribing his tapes and putting in his revisions, Jenna had wondered where he got his information.

Perhaps he'd given her a clue just now. He was a reader. He'd probably been inspired by something he read. Given the subject of his book, she assumed that he read and enjoyed espionage thrillers.

"I need to jot down the new scene that came to me before I forget it," he said and left as silently as he arrived. Once he was gone, Jenna became hypnotized once again by the sound of his deep voice rumbling in her ear.

By Friday morning she was exhausted, listening to the tapes and trying to understand what he wanted to say. He must have been distracted or in pain or *some*thing because she had never heard him so disjointed. He mumbled. He backtracked. Worse than that, he must have reverted to pacing as he talked because he didn't always talk into the microphone. She could pick up a few words before the rest faded away.

The strain of trying to make out what he was saying gave her a pounding headache.

About an hour into her work schedule, Jenna tossed her earphones down with a muted shriek. Now he sounded as though he were speaking Chinese…in gale-force winds.

Definitely time for a break before she tossed the tapes across the room in frustration.

As she left her office she saw Hazel in the hall.

"You look upset. Are you all right?" Hazel asked.

"Not really, no."

"Want to talk about it?"

"I was headed to the kitchen for tea if you care to join me."

Hazel waited until they were seated at the small table in the dining room alcove with steaming cups of tea in front of them before she asked, "Is this about Ian?"

Jenna sighed. "Not really. I'm tired, that's all. I could definitely use a break."

"Then take one. He's not an ogre, you know."

Jenna chuckled. "I know. He's been working longer hours and I've been doing my best to keep up with him. I wonder if he's getting any sleep at all! I guess I'm feeling a little overwhelmed today, that's all."

"You aren't going to quit, are you?" Hazel asked, looking worried. "The problem with Ian is that he's not good with people. He tries, of course. It seems to me that no matter how well things are going for him, he has a knack for shooting himself in the foot when he has to deal with others."

"Maybe that's what's wrong with his leg. He missed his original target." Their eyes met and they broke out laughing. Jenna wiped tears from her eyes when she'd calmed down, and shook her head. "I can't believe I said that. I'm more tired than I thought."

Hazel reached into her pocket and pulled out a set of car keys. "Here. Take my car and go somewhere for the weekend. Now that I think about it, you haven't had a weekend off since you came. No wonder you're close to burnout."

"You're right. I do need to get away." Jenna sighed. "I hate to disturb him in case he's finally resting but I need to let him know that I'm leaving."

"Don't worry about it. If he asks about you, I'll tell him you took the weekend off. The weather seems to be improving. You can explore, visit some shops…have fun."

"Actually, I might pursue my search for a man."

Hazel's eyebrows lifted. "You don't say," she replied, amused.

Jenna chuckled. "Nothing like that. Someone

from Scotland was looking for me last winter. I didn't hear about it until I arrived in the U.K. The name he gave, if my informant was correct, was Dumas. She said he sounded like an American.''

"Did your informant say where in Scotland he was from?"

"Edinburgh. He isn't listed with the telephone company there, though. Since I didn't spend much time there when I first arrived, I may go back to see what I can find out."

"Do you have any idea why he was looking for you?"

"No. I was hoping it had something to do with my being adopted."

"Adopted! You don't say. Well, I can certainly see why you're curious to meet him. Would your adopted parents know him, by chance?"

"Somehow I doubt it. They died many years ago, while I was a child."

"I'm sorry to hear that. Well, you go have your search and enjoy yourself."

"Thank you, Hazel. Whatever Ian pays you, it isn't nearly enough. You've made my stay here very pleasant."

"I'll tell him you said that. Don't worry about Ian. He probably won't notice you're gone. He's been immersed in his book so much he sometimes forgets to eat."

While on her way to Edinburgh, Jenna mapped out a plan of sorts. She would check with surrounding towns for the mysterious Mr. Dumas as well as explore.

Although she had no luck in her search, she enjoyed touring the castles and other historical buildings in the area. While she was away, she went to bed early and slept late so that by Sunday evening when she returned to the castle, she was feeling more rested. With more rest, reason returned. By detaching herself somewhat from her situation with Ian, she could see the humor in the situation…that is, until she found a note lying on top of the computer keyboard in Ian's handwriting stating, ''Please see me at your convenience.''

''I knew I should have gone directly to my room and not checked the office tonight,'' she muttered to herself.

She went in search of Hazel and found her in the kitchen.

''Ah, there you are, looking oh so much better,'' Hazel said, smiling. ''Didn't I tell you? Just what you needed.''

Jenna smiled. ''I was feeling the same way until I found this on the computer just now,'' she said, handing Hazel the note. ''So much for his not being aware I was gone.''

''It does him good to discover that you're an employee and not a slave…and that's just what I told him when he came searching for you on Friday.''

''Friday! Oh, no,'' Jenna said with a groan. ''I'd

hoped he wouldn't miss me until yesterday at the earliest.''

Hazel's lips twitched at her reaction. "Actually he came looking for you about an hour after you left, as it happens."

Jenna absently accepted a cup of tea from her. "Thank you." She took a sip and asked, "Where do you think I could find him at this hour?"

"His rooms, probably. I'll show you where they are after you've had your tea. Go on, sit down and tell me about your search for the unknown man."

Jenna sat. She didn't suppose a few minutes would make much difference in the general scheme of things.

"I ended up staying one night in Edinburgh and spent the rest of the time visiting charming towns and villages in the surrounding area. I looked in the telephone directory of each one in hopes of finding Mr. Dumas listed. I had no luck."

"I know you're disappointed. Other than that, did you enjoy getting out and about?"

"Oh, yes. I enjoyed the countryside. I was amazed at the large number of sheep."

"You find that unusual?" Hazel asked. "Australia is known for the number of sheep there."

"Yes, well, they weren't wandering the streets of Sydney, so I had never seen so many before."

"Stands to reason, I suppose," Hazel replied. She took a sip of her tea and without looking at Jenna, asked, "I can't help but be curious, Jenna. Do you find Ian the least bit attractive?"

Jenna stared at the housekeeper in surprise. "Why would you ask such a thing?"

"Just wondered, is all. I was thinking about how much he's come out of his shell since you came. There are times when he appears quite affable, although I wished for my camera to have captured his expression when I told him you were gone. He was positively ashen before I told him you'd be back sometime over the weekend."

"He probably couldn't bear the thought of hiring yet another secretary if I didn't come back," Jenna said, chuckling.

"I notice you didn't answer my question."

Jenna didn't answer right away. "I suppose I do find him attractive," she finally replied. She eyed Hazel. "You aren't by any chance trying to play matchmaker, are you?"

"Of course not! I wouldn't think of it." Hazel stood and picked up her cup without meeting Jenna's eyes. "I was curious if you find him intimidating or formidable, or if you're able to see beneath his gruff surface."

"He has many admirable qualities. His determination and persistence in both his recovery and his work impress me." There was no way she would admit to having erotic dreams about him!

A short while later she followed Hazel's directions until she found his rooms. He was on the ground floor, which made sense, given his injuries.

She stopped in front of his door, took a deep breath and knocked. There was no sound after she knocked and Jenna was surprised when the door abruptly swung open.

"Good evening, Ian. You said—"

"Come in." After the briefest of pauses, he added, "Please."

Jenna stepped into the sitting room and looked around. The place looked quite comfortable with its oversize furniture and bookshelves crammed with books. A fire danced in the fireplace.

She turned and looked at him, waiting for his reprimand for not checking with him before she left for the weekend. She tilted her head slightly and asked, "You wanted to see me?"

"Yes, but it can wait. I've been toying with an idea that I believe will help to explain some of Philip's later actions and I wanted to get your opinion. However, we can discuss the book later." He nodded to a grouping of chairs in front of the fire. "Come and sit, if you will."

She crossed the room, feeling awkward. All of their meetings had taken place in the library or her office. Being here in his private quarters made their meeting seem more personal somehow. She probably wouldn't be feeling so self-conscious if Hazel's earlier remarks would stop tumbling around in her head.

Once seated across from him, she waited for him to speak. What was the matter with him? He was the one who wanted to see her. She wished he'd say whatever was on his mind and let her go to bed. Uh, to her room to go to bed, she mentally corrected.

But he said nothing more.

After waiting what she considered to be long enough, Jenna said, "You said you wanted to see me. I'm here. Say something."

"Where did you go?"

Whatever she'd been expecting him to say, that wasn't it. She smiled and said lightly, "Exploring."

"Why?"

Maybe he was sleep deprived and his brain wasn't hitting on all cylinders. "Because I enjoy exploring?" she replied, using a slightly questioning tone.

"Were you interviewing for another job?"

She stiffened. "Of course not. Am I supposed to be?"

"Hazel informed me yesterday that I was well on the path to driving you away."

"Ah."

"What do you mean by that?"

"Very little, actually. Is this your way of telling me that you wish me to continue working for you?"

"Of course I want you to continue with your job."

"Then you aren't angry that I left without telling you."

"No. I've been working you too hard."

"Another one of Hazel's quotes?"

He flushed. "Yes." He seemed to take an inordinate amount of interest in the fire. Eventually, he said, " According to Hazel you've been working nonstop since you arrived."

"Hazel is just full of information, isn't she?"

"I don't want you to think of me as a slave driver."

She didn't respond immediately. Instead, she studied his face with its lines and planes. He wasn't model handsome, of course. He looked too rugged and world-weary for that. It didn't detract from his attractiveness, though. She had a sudden urge to get up and walk behind him so that she could massage his neck and shoulders. She had never seen him in quite this mood before. He looked tired.

"How much more do you have to do to finish your book?" she asked.

As though picking up on her thoughts, Ian rubbed the back of his neck. "Two or three scenes, I guess. It should be finished in a few weeks."

"I know you'll be happy to have it finished."

He nodded. "The revisions won't take as much of your time as the transcribing does."

"That's true."

"I'll still need your help, though."

She smiled. "I'll be here until you have no further use for my services." She stood and he came to his feet, as well. He didn't wince at the movement, she noticed. His knee was definitely improving.

She was almost to the door when he said, "Would you like to have dinner with me tomorrow night?"

Jenna turned and smiled. "I would like that very much. Thank you." She opened the door.

"I meant here. At the castle. I don't like going out much."

"That will be fine." She closed the door behind her.

Ian stared at the door for several minutes before he placed the screen in front of the fire and went to his bedroom.

Hazel had been right—Jenna hadn't left without notice as he'd first thought.

When he'd discovered she was gone he had come close to panicking. He'd grown used to discussing his progress on the book with her. He'd found her comments and suggestions invaluable.

His early decision to stay away from her had soon disappeared. He'd found it impossible to resist her fresh-faced beauty and happy disposition. She'd taken over his dreams, causing him to wake up shaken and alone. He'd been telling himself that it wasn't because of her, personally. His reaction to her merely emphasized his need for female companionship. With her unexpected departure, he'd faced the truth. He didn't want just any woman. He wanted Jenna.

His dilemma was…what did he intend to do about it?

Chapter Six

Jenna awoke early the next morning. Her first thought was about Ian's unexpected dinner invitation.

She smiled to herself and stretched. She'd seen a different side to him last night, one she found to be quite charming.

She was still smiling when she went downstairs for breakfast. When Cook saw her, she said, "You're up early, lass. Breakfast will be ready shortly."

"There's no rush. I must have caught up on my sleep over the weekend. Since I awoke early, I decided to enjoy the early-morning sun."

"If you intend to spend time outside, you'd better

do it soon. We're expecting a thunderstorm later today.''

"Really? The only weather I've seen since I moved to Scotland is sunshine, clouds and rain. I didn't realize you were subject to heavy storms.''

"The electrical storms come charging through more often in the spring. It has to do with the cold and warm air mixing it up, I'm told.''

Jenna poured herself a cup of coffee and walked over to one of the windows. At the moment everything looked quite warm and sunny. Hopefully she could wander in the gardens for a while before clouds moved into the area.

After breakfast she went outside to see what had been done while she was away. The groundskeepers were in the process of loosening the soil in preparation for the spring plants grown in the greenhouse.

There were faint signs that the trees were ready to don their spring attire of soft green. She'd fallen in love with country living and hoped that once she left here she would be able to find other work outside a large city. She'd discovered that nature was full of surprises. She was never bored watching as the seasons continued their cycle.

After following her usual route Jenna decided to walk down the lane to the main road. Her discussion with Ian last night kept surfacing in her mind. He'd come close to an apology, which she felt certain was unusual. Perhaps that was why he preferred to keep to himself. Fewer apologies that way.

His suggestion that they have dinner together was definitely out of character. Jenna had difficulty visualizing a meal with Ian as the genial host. At the very least, the evening should provide entertainment.

Later, Jenna approached the entrance to the courtyard and saw Hazel coming toward her.

"Beautiful day, isn't it?" Jenna asked when she spotted Hazel.

"I suppose. I hadn't really noticed." Hazel looked up at the sky. "Don't expect the sun to last long, though. We have quite a blow charging our way."

"I took a walk to the end of the lane. The trees must be beautiful with their full greenery."

"I'm glad you like the country. I was afraid you'd become bored so far from a city."

"Not at all. Sometimes I feel that I've always lived here. It's strange, really. I never felt I belonged when I lived in Sydney. I figured it was because I had no family there. Yet here I am without family and feeling that the hills and rolling pastures are familiar somehow."

"Ian tells me the two of you are having dinner together tonight. I believe that he's trying to make up for his antisocial behavior since you've been here." Hazel chuckled. "It's about time he noticed, don't you think?"

"He told me last night that he was sorry for the way he's been behaving. You must have given him quite a tongue-lashing, which I consider quite brave of you, considering some of his moods.''

"Ian's been too absorbed in his recovery and his writing these past months. It's time he gets out more. He needs to be socialized before he becomes a permanent beast, rather than just a wounded one,'' Hazel replied, ''and so I told him.''

Hazel turned back toward the castle and over her shoulder said, ''Dinner is at eight.''

Jenna tried not to spend any more time thinking about the upcoming evening. Ian probably thought she was having hot flashes when she blushed every time he walked into her office. If he only knew the erotic dreams she had about him, he'd be blushing, too!

Until Hazel started probing about Jenna finding him attractive, Jenna had not allowed herself to think of her dreams as being anything more than fantasies, such as ones she might have about a cinema star.

She had never had an intimate relationship because she'd never been tempted to get sexually involved with anyone she'd dated. As a result, Jenna had concluded she wasn't the type to feel passion.

If her dreams were any indication, she had more passion buried in her subconscious than was comfortable. She gave her head a brief shake and went inside. Perhaps concentrating on work would help to clear her mind.

Ian stared into the mirror, a frown on his face. His dinner invitation last night had been impulsive and he'd been pleased that she had accepted. Now he had to spend time with her on a social level, which was far different from their casual, friendly working relationship. He'd never been good at social chitchat. To spend more time with Jenna, though, he was willing to make the effort.

He probably owed Hazel thanks for forcing him to look at the situation. Ian smiled reluctantly. Hazel had never pulled her punches so there was no reason to be upset with her. He respected anyone who held his or her ground. Jenna made it clear from their first meeting that she wouldn't back down from an altercation.

The truth was, he felt inept when it came time for him to play host. His mother often lamented to anyone who would listen while he was growing up about how difficult it was to train him in rudimentary social skills.

His father had consoled him more than once after his mother had pointed out his duty as a MacGowan to mingle with others. His father understood how he felt and sympathized, but he'd also told him that the fact remained that Ian's mother was right.

As he grew older, Ian became more subtle in dodging and escaping the large gatherings he was expected to attend. His mother had seen through his flimsy excuses, pointing out that subtlety was not his strong suit.

A few years ago, his mother had gleefully relinquished to Hazel her role as his social nag. On more than one occasion he'd reminded Hazel that as her employer he deserved a little more respect and a good deal less harassment from her…a sentiment she ignored without hesitation.

Perhaps he would draw Jenna out and get her to talk about herself. That way he wouldn't be expected to spend much time in conversation.

Jenna had been there for almost three months and the truth of the matter was that he knew very little about her. Didn't he want to learn more about the woman who disturbed his dreams and destroyed many a night's rest?

Ian slipped on his jacket and took one last look in the mirror. He reminded himself of everything his mother had taught him through the years. If ever there was a time to put them to practice, it was now.

Jenna looked through her wardrobe for something appropriate to wear for dinner with the laird of the castle. Her wardrobe did not lend itself to social events. Instead, her closet contained clothes suitable for work.

She began to panic when she went through her choices and nothing looked promising. Starting over, she took each garment out and looked at it more critically. That's when she spotted at the back of the closet a dress she'd forgotten she owned. The color was cobalt blue, with a V-neck and straight skirt that stopped at the knee.

She'd bought the dress on sale several months ago and had never before had an occasion to wear it. Tonight offered an opportunity that might not come her way again anytime soon.

Before she left the room Jenna took a moment to look at herself in the mirror. She had to admit, if only to herself, that the dress was flattering to her fair skin and reddish-blond hair. She'd left her hair down tonight, surprised to see how long it had gotten. It fell in waves to her shoulders, giving her a look that was not at all familiar.

The strappy heels she'd bought to go with the ensemble appeared frivolous and impractical—just the look she'd hoped to achieve when she'd purchased them.

With a renewed sense of self-confidence Jenna went downstairs. The library was empty and she went to look for Ian in the dining room, which turned out to be empty, as well.

Jenna decided to look more closely at some of the paintings while she waited for Ian. She willed her shoulders to relax in an effort to appear calm.

The large, formal portrait that hung at the end of the room facing the head of the table had fascinated her since the first time she'd seen it. The woman in the painting looked regal, wrapped in the Mac-Gowan tartan with a fortune in jewels on her neck, ears and fingers. She had the fair skin and bright blue eyes Jenna associated with native Scots.

The woman's light brown hair curled around her ears in a most becoming manner. She was quite beautiful and yet it was her expression that intrigued Jenna. She seemed so full of joy and life, her smile on the verge of becoming a mischievous grin.

Jenna wondered which ancestor of Ian's this was.

As though reading her mind, Ian said from somewhere behind her, "My mother." Startled, she spun around and fought to hang on to her composure when she saw him.

He stood in the doorway wearing a black jacket, a white shirt and the MacGowan plaid, the kilt revealing muscled legs covered with woolen stockings. The fact that the shirt was open at the collar in no way detracted from the formal and striking figure he made.

He'd brushed his hair away from his face, the light emphasizing the planes and angles of his face. The custom-made jacket drew attention to his broad shoulders.

Oh, my. He looked absolutely gorgeous in a rugged sort of way and the thoughts that immediately popped into her head were much too earthy to be shared.

"Your mother is quite beautiful," she said, forcibly reminding herself to stop staring at him. She turned back to the portrait instead.

"Yes," he replied, moving to stand beside her,

"she always has been." She glanced at him in time
to see his lips curl at the corners into a smile. "Dad
still complains that she attracts a bevy of men wherever they go."

"Where do your parents live?"

"When Dad retired, they decided to move to the
south of France to get away from our winters. That
left me to look after this monstrous pile of rocks."
She heard the affection in his voice when he spoke
of the castle. "They returned after I was injured and
stayed several weeks before I convinced them I was
well on the way to recovery. Mother has a tendency
to hover, you see.

"Shall we be seated?" Ian asked. He nodded toward the table where someone had set two places,
one at the end and the other to the right. "I'll admit
that I'm somewhat rusty at being a host."

"It was kind of you to invite me. I hope this isn't
an inconvenience for you."

His smile was so unexpected that she could only
stare at him when he replied. "Not at all. It's past
time that we became better acquainted. I know very
little about you other than you're an excellent assistant."

He paused behind her chair and pulled it away
from the table for her.

"Thank you," she said, then watched as he seated
himself. "I doubt you'd find my history particularly
interesting."

He looked at her with a raised brow. "I sincerely

hope you'll allow me to decide whether I find you interesting.''

She almost corrected him. She'd suggested that her history might—oh bother. She wondered if the meal would be filled with miscommunications? If so, it was going to be a long evening.

He was probably entertaining himself by deliberately misunderstanding.

''You look quite different tonight,'' he said after a long silence. She could practically feel his gaze touching her everywhere he looked. She swallowed. ''I don't recall seeing your hair like that before,'' he added.

''I prefer wearing it up when I'm at work.''

''Ah.''

Another long silence fell between them before Hazel brought in their first course. They ate in silence until Hazel had served the second course, when Ian cleared his throat and said, ''You should wear that color more often. It's very becoming on you.''

Jenna suddenly became fascinated with the food on her plate. ''Thank you,'' she finally said, knowing she was blushing. Darn her fair skin, anyway.

''I'm sorry if I embarrassed you,'' he said, confirming that he'd noticed.

''That's all right. I'm not used to people paying me compliments.'' She glanced over and saw that he was staring at her in surprise.

''I find that difficult to believe. You're a very

beautiful woman, Jenna. Are you saying no one has ever told you that?''

Jenna carefully lay her knife and fork down, no longer pretending to eat. She forced herself to meet his gaze. ''No,'' she said starkly.

''Unbelievable. I would have thought—'' He paused. ''Never mind,'' he said, picking up his glass of wine and taking a long swallow.

''It's all right. What were you going to say?''

''Didn't your parents—'' he began, then stopped and shook his head, refusing to continue.

''I was brought up in an orphanage.''

''Well. That was certainly inept of me. I apologize,'' he said stiffly.

He looked so miserable sitting there that she impulsively reached over and touched his fingers with her own. ''How would you have known? I lost my parents many years ago. In fact, I barely remember them. Looks were never discussed when I was growing up, except to make sure I was clean and had combed my hair.'' She touched a lock of her hair and smiled. ''I wore my hair much shorter then. It made it easier to care for.''

He clasped her hand and leaned forward. ''I had no idea. I feel sorry for the little girl you once were. We're going to have to do something about getting you used to compliments.''

Just then Hazel came in with their dessert, smiling when she saw him leaning toward Jenna, holding her hand.

They jumped apart as though caught doing something illicit.

Hazel said, "The wind's picking up out there. Radio says the storm has already caused some damage in its path. Hope we only get the edge of it."

Ian nodded without looking at either woman. Jenna looked at her plate and discovered she had scarcely touched her food.

"Everything has been delicious," she said. "Please tell Cook that she outdid herself this evening."

"The best compliment you could pay her is to eat what's on your plate." Jenna jerked up her head and looked at Hazel in surprise. Hazel's eyes danced and she added, "Otherwise, you might not get any dessert."

"You might as well do what she says," Ian said with mock resignation. "Hazel has some very strict rules."

He was actually teasing, Jenna thought in wonderment. Her view of the man continued to need adjusting as the meal progressed.

Relaxing for the first time since Ian had walked into the room, Jenna picked up her utensils and began to eat. Since Ian hadn't eaten much more than she had, he followed her example, causing Hazel to laugh out loud.

"All right, children. I'll be back to make certain you don't eat your dessert prematurely."

She strode out of the room, leaving Ian and Jenna

staring at each other. Ian began to laugh and Jenna soon joined him. He had an infectious laugh that rumbled through his chest. She had never heard him laugh before. Tonight was filled with surprises!

"Do I need to apologize for my housekeeper's manners?" he finally asked.

Jenna shook her head. "Absolutely not. I adore the woman, although I'm not used to being referred to as a child."

"You're not! How about me? I have ten years on you."

They smiled at each other in mutual understanding.

The silence no longer bothered her and when she reached for her dessert, Jenna chuckled, thinking of Hazel.

"I'm quite curious to know your occupation before your auto accident."

"Oh, I'm one of those office drones that works for the government," he replied easily.

She smiled. An accountant, no doubt. He probably knows someone who works as a government agent, she thought, in order to get what appeared to be accurate details of what they do.

Hazel walked in. "I thought you might want to have coffee in the library," she said.

"Good idea," he replied. He stood and held out his hand to Jenna as Hazel said, "The storm is much closer. We can hear the thunder rolling in. Thought I'd warn you."

They left the dining room and Jenna said, "She's brought up the storm more than once today. Why would she feel the need to warn you about it?"

"Because every time we have a bit of a blow—" the lights went off, leaving them in the dark "—the lights go out," he finished with a sigh. His hand brushed hers and he took it in a firm grip. "Although the antiquated wiring is adequate most of the time, the transformer generally gives out soon after a storm hits. I have oil lamps in the library. We should be all right."

When they walked into the room Jenna noticed that the drapes over the French doors hadn't been pulled. She could see the trees being lashed by the wind. The sky lit up, giving them light to walk to the chairs where Hazel had set the coffee service.

Jenna shuddered as she listened to the wind whistling and the rain beating down on the stone terrace.

Thunder crashed again before the lightning faded away. "That one's close," she said nervously. "Do you have storms like this often?"

"Thankfully, not too often." He led her to one of the chairs facing the fireplace, where the flames danced and swirled as air blew down through the chimney.

Jenna looked around. "We really don't need additional light at the moment, do we? Between the fire and the lightning we could almost read a newspaper in here."

She watched Ian remove his jacket and roll up his

shirtsleeves. "There. I hope you don't mind but I wear a formal jacket as seldom as possible." He chose the chair closest to her and sat. When she reached for the coffee carafe, he said, "Here, let me. You do what you can to relax." He smiled at her, the light from the fireplace gilding his face. "Keep in mind that this place has weathered many a storm in the past three hundred years, so you needn't fear it will come tumbling down around our ears." He paused. "The dry rot will do that." When he saw her expression, he burst into laughter. Again. "That's a joke. We somehow manage to stay ahead of the dry rot."

She found this new Ian fascinating. She saw no sign of the gruff, taciturn man she'd thought she knew. How unfair of him to show such a charming side while she was already battling her strong attraction to him.

Some alchemy had taken place tonight, changing the often grim and silent man into a thoughtful, considerate and kind one. His discomfort earlier when he learned of her childhood had shown her a gentle side to him she would never have believed existed.

Now here he was, pouring her coffee and teasing her into relaxing despite the storm.

She'd never liked thunderstorms—hated them, in fact. If she were alone she'd be huddled in bed with the covers over her head and her hands over her ears just as she'd always done as a child.

Her parents had died in a thunderstorm.

She cleared her throat. "Before coming here, I'd never given a thought to the amount of maintenance it takes to keep centuries-old buildings."

"It could be worse, I suppose," Ian replied. "Some castles near the coast get water in the lower floors whenever a storm blows in, no matter what they do. All we've had to deal with is dry rot, temperamental plumbing and obsolete wiring."

She laughed. "Goodness. That sounds daunting."

"At times it can be, but it's my heritage and I respect that. There's been a MacGowan living here for many generations."

Feeling wistful, she said, "How reassuring to know your lineage."

"Don't you have someone in your extended family who could tell you about yours?"

"I thought I did, which is one of the reasons I came to the U.K. That's when I discovered that I'd been adopted. It seems there's no one to ask to find out anything about my original family."

"The news must have been quite a shock for you."

"I was devastated, actually." She told him briefly about her childhood in Australia, her trip to Cornwall and her visit with Morwenna Hoskins. "The only thing I discovered during that visit was that a man by the name of Dumas from Edinburgh had come looking in Cornwall for me. At the time, I considered the news to be a sign that I should come to Scotland. However, when I could find no trace of him once I arrived, I realized how childish I'd been, hoping to find a father or brother or some other close relative.''

''So that's why you're here. I've been curious about that…that someone with your skills would be willing to bury herself in the country with little outside entertainment. If you'd like, I can see what I can find out for you. I have a few contacts that might be able to help.''

Ian went over to a cabinet and retrieved a bottle of brandy. Picking up a couple of balloon-shaped glasses, he returned to where she sat. He poured the liquid into the glasses and handed her one.

''Oh! You would be willing to do that?'' she asked, after thanking him for the drink.

''I'm not making any promises, mind you, but I'll see what I can do.''

They sat quietly, until Jenna, feeling that she wasn't keeping up with her end of the conversation, said, ''I notice that you're doing quite well without your cane.''

''For which I'm thankful, although some days are better than others. For instance, I didn't need Hazel to tell me about the upcoming storm. My leg's been sending urgent messages for several hours.''

''What do you intend to do when the book is finished?''

''Send it to one of the men I work with. His father is a publisher. I spoke with Craig not long ago to see if he would be willing to read the manuscript and let me know if he thought his father might be interested in it.''

''You intend to return to your government job, now that you're doing so well?''

''Hopefully, yes. I need to arrange a meeting with my supervisor.''

She smiled. ''Todd something? He was the person you thought had sent me to you, as I recall.''

''You would have to remind me of that, of course. I was being rather high-handed that day, as I recall. I have no excuse for my boorish behavior.''

''I believe your disposition suffers when you're in a great deal of pain.''

''That's very generous of you to say so. If you don't mind, I'll borrow that excuse whenever I'm being particularly revolting.''

She laughed. ''I'll manage to overlook your moods.'' After a sip of her brandy, she asked, ''Will you live in London once you return to work?''

''Yes.''

''I don't know how you can bear leaving here. I've enjoyed my stay here and have grown quite attached to the place.''

A sudden clap of thunder shook the glass in the windows and Jenna instantly cringed, her brandy sloshing in its glass. Forcing herself to focus on the conversation—and hoping that he hadn't noticed her fear—Jenna said lightly, ''Since you won't need a secretary in London, I'll need to update my résumé and contact Ms. Spradlin soon.''

"Not necessarily," he said.

"I would have nothing to do after you move to London."

"You could move there, as well, you know."

She looked sharply at him, surprised by his suggestion. Surely he wasn't serious. "I prefer the country," she replied lightly. "No doubt Ms. Spradlin will be able to find me another position with no problem, or so she led me to believe."

He didn't say anything and she lapsed into silence, as well, enjoying her time with Ian, despite the storm. Being there with him helped her to hold her fears at bay.

Eventually the storm slackened, the thunder occurring less frequently and the rain nothing more than a gentle sound in the room. She glanced at her watch and was surprised to discover it was close to midnight. The evening had flown and she was pleased to have seen this side of Ian. She had enjoyed his company.

She yawned and hastily covered her mouth. "I'm sorry. I hadn't realized it was so late. It's way past my bedtime."

He looked equally surprised. "Oh. I'm sorry. I'm so used to staying up until all hours that I didn't give the time a thought. Allow me to walk you home," he said, rising and holding out his hand to her.

Without thinking, she took it, feeling the comforting warmth on her icy fingers.

"You're freezing! Why haven't you said something?"

"It's all right. It's mostly my hands."

He took them between his and rubbed them, imparting his warmth to her. Just then a belated crack of thunder rumbled across the sky, as though taking one last stab at the area before leaving. Jenna jumped and shivered despite her best efforts at control.

"You really don't like storms, do you?" he asked gently.

"Not particularly, no."

He put his arm around her and walked her out of the room. The hall was black.

"We need some light," she said.

"I have a penlight that will do," he replied, reaching into a pocket hidden in the folds of his kilt.

"I hate to ask you to walk up the stairs. Why don't I light one of the lamps in the library instead?"

"You didn't ask. I volunteered. Besides, walking your date to her door is expected of a gentleman." He briefly hugged her closer to his side.

"Is this a date?" she asked, suddenly unable to get her breath.

He stopped on the stairway and looked at her. Although his light guided their footsteps, she couldn't see the expression on his face.

"It has seemed that way," he replied with a hint of surprise. "I've enjoyed the evening very much,

Jenna. Thank you for having dinner with me.'' He continued up the stairs. Once they reached the upper hallway he guided her toward her room.

The windows along the gallery lit up with flickering lightning some distance away. Ian said, ''This reminds me of many a stormy night when I was a lad. I'd have friends over for the night whenever we expected to have a storm. We'd do our best to scare one another witless by hiding and jumping out as someone walked by. It was great fun,'' he added, ''although I believe some of the maids complained.''

''I haven't seen any of your friends since I've been here.''

''Most of them have drifted away. The only one I keep in close contact with is Chris Wood. He's an attorney and at the moment is away in Germany negotiating some large contract for a client.''

This close to Ian, she could hear him breathe, feel his reassuring warmth and was highly sensitive to the touch of his arm brushing against hers.

She was relieved when they reached her room without her making a complete fool of herself. Ian turned to her and gently touched her hair with his free hand as though unable to resist.

''Sweet dreams, Jenna,'' he said, and lowered his head.

He gave her plenty of time to step away to avoid his kiss if she wanted but she didn't move. Perhaps he intended to brush his lips across hers and walk away, but that wasn't what happened.

As soon as their lips touched, a blazing inferno engulfed them, so incendiary that Jenna could only hold him tightly so she wouldn't collapse. She gave herself over to whatever forces within her had been waiting for this moment.

Jenna went up on tiptoe and wrapped her arms around his neck. Her surrender encouraged him to pull her more tightly against him, his mouth moving over hers as though he was memorizing the taste and shape of her lips.

She had no idea how long the kiss lasted, but when Ian finally withdrew his mouth from hers they were both trembling and breathing harshly.

As though coming out of a trance, Ian seemed to realize what he had done and immediately released her. "I'm sorry," he said hoarsely. "I didn't mean to— I shouldn't have— Please forgive me," he finally managed to say as though expecting a slap at any moment.

She touched the irresistible cleft in his chin with her finger. "You owe me no apologies, Ian. Surely you were aware of my wholehearted participation."

"I don't want you to feel that I'm taking advantage of you, living under my roof. That's the very last thing I want," he said stiffly, and she realized he'd withdrawn into himself once more.

She stroked his cheek, feeling the loss of the man she'd spent the evening with. "Good night, Ian," she said, and stepped back into her room. For one insane moment before she shut the door she wanted to invite him inside.

The thought shocked her. She knew that she would never view Ian MacGowan in the same way again.

Chapter Seven

Jenna heard the rain before she fully awoke the next morning. She lay in bed and listened to the steady tapping on the windowpanes.

She was in a new place, emotionally speaking, a place she'd never been. The employer she thought she knew had become a different person last night, a person who generally hid behind a cold, abrupt demeanor, and she longed to get to know him.

The kiss they'd shared had been far from cold…or abrupt. Jenna had drifted into her room last night caught up in her heightened emotions, trembling with need to complete what they had started. Their kiss had caused her erotic dreams and the emotions they had evoked to pale in comparison.

Once in bed she lay awake for what seemed like hours, reliving those moments of being plastered against his body, his arousal silent acknowledgment that he was as affected by the kiss as she.

Now she had to go downstairs and treat Ian as though nothing out of the ordinary had happened.

Jenna felt more vulnerable than ever.

Once dressed, she went downstairs to breakfast.

Cook was in the alcove, placing coffee, juice and muffins on the table. "Good morning!" she said cheerfully. "You'll be pleased to know that we have electricity once again. Ian said he's not going to postpone another day requesting an estimate to replace the wiring. Who knows? It's possible we may catch up with the twentieth century now that we're into the twenty-first!"

After breakfast, Jenna went to her office to go to work.

Ian had been there sometime that morning. A marked-up copy of a stack of pages she had transcribed was there, as well as one tape with a note attached. She sat and stared at the note. "This is the last one!" Ian had written with a flourish. "It's all downhill from here."

He signed it with his initial as he always did. There was absolutely no reason for her heart to be racing. Why was she being so silly? She was more than a little irritated with herself.

Jenna briskly inserted the tape, adjusted her earphones and immediately began to type.

She had a habit of listening and typing with her eyes closed. The scenes came alive for her and she became caught up in the story. A few hours later Jenna felt a presence in the room and opened her eyes. Ian stood in front of the desk, looking at her with a bemused expression on his face.

She removed the earphones and asked warily, "Did you want something?" Jenna felt the fiery red of embarrassment sweep over her when she realized how her question had sounded.

Thankfully he didn't appear to notice. "Not really. I was wondering if you intended to stop for lunch."

She glanced at her watch and was surprised to discover it was after one o'clock. "Oh. I didn't realize the time."

He smiled somewhat shyly. "You seemed engrossed and I couldn't decide whether or not to interrupt you. I didn't want to startle you." His warm gaze kept her blush in place and she was thankful he pretended not to notice. "I'd made up my mind to retreat when you opened your eyes."

She stood and stretched. "I'll go see what Cook has available," she said.

"I, uh, asked her if she would do up some sandwiches and things. I thought I'd invite you to join me in the library for an indoor picnic, considering the damp weather."

Oh, dear. The way he was looking at her was causing her to respond to his presence as she had the night before. She couldn't find her tongue to give him a sensible answer. How ridiculous could she be? He'd suggested a picnic together, not a lovers' tryst. "I would enjoy that," she replied, feeling shy.

His grin was her reward for agreeing, she thought, fascinated by the curve of his mouth, the sensuousness of his lips, the— "I'll, uh, just go freshen up and meet you in the library," she said before fleeing his presence.

After taking time to regain her composure, Jenna went into the library and saw that Ian had been serious about an actual picnic. He'd spread a blanket in front of the fire and had placed a plate of sandwiches and other mouthwatering items there.

She found him stretched out on his side, his hand propping up his head, waiting for her. As soon as he saw her, he said, "Hope this isn't too casual for you." He had an amused gleam in his eyes as though expecting her to object.

She sat as gracefully as possible across from him. "This is fine," she said. "What made you think of it?"

He started to answer, then stopped. With a diffidence she wouldn't have believed possible, he said, "I wanted to see you again...spend some time with you that didn't involve work. I hope you don't mind."

She couldn't help but ask, "Are you feeling all right?"

He raised his brows. "Am I acting out of character?"

She relaxed and smiled at him. "A little, perhaps, but I could easily get used to this new Ian," she said lightly, reaching for a carrot stick.

"I discovered something quite important last night."

"Oh?" She eyed him warily.

"I'm not the recluse I thought I was. I enjoyed our evening…immensely, I might add. I thought that once the weather clears I'd like to take you to one of my favorite places. It's perhaps an hour's drive from here but it's well worth the time."

"Well, I—" She waved her hand vaguely toward her office. "I thought you wanted—"

"Oh, I know you're wondering about the book. From what I could tell, you're almost finished with the last tape, aren't you?"

She grinned, feeling a little sheepish. "As a matter of fact, I am. I was caught off guard by your plot twist at the end. I never saw it coming."

"Something else I thought of last night after I returned to my room. I realized that getting away from the story for a few hours gave me a slightly different perspective on how I wanted to end it. So you like it?"

"Very much. I'm on the epilogue at the moment."

"You see? You're almost done."

"Your marked revisions need to be added."

"All right. Perhaps the weather will clear by to-morrow."

Jenna filled two plates with food and handed him one. She poured steaming tea into their cups and settled in to eat, a sense of pleasure settling over her.

She wished that he had opened up sooner instead of at the end of her stay there. For the first time since she arrived, Jenna realized that she was going to miss Ian very much once she moved on to her next position.

"What are you thinking?" he asked suddenly, breaking the silence.

"Why do you ask?"

"I was watching the various expressions on your face and became curious."

"Oh." She wondered how much to tell him. "Well," she said slowly, "I was thinking that I would enjoy seeing the countryside with you...and that I'm glad I came to work for you."

After a lengthy pause, Ian quietly replied, "So am I."

Chapter Eight

"I promise not to make another change to this thing," Ian said, walking into Jenna's office one afternoon in the middle of June. "I apologize for pushing you so hard the last couple of weeks in order to get the manuscript ready to mail."

"I haven't minded." She pointed to a stack of pages beside the computer. "I'm caught up with you. There's a chance I could mail this today, if you'd like."

Since their impromptu picnic a few weeks before, she and Ian had spent more time together. When she went downstairs each morning he would be waiting for her and they would breakfast together.

He appeared more relaxed these days. The frown

was gone—most of the time—although he hadn't suddenly become a new person. He was still impatient and abrupt sometimes, but his moods no longer bothered her. In fact, she ignored them.

By some unspoken agreement, they never discussed what happened between them the night of the storm. Jenna was relieved not to have Ian explain the episode away as though kissing her had meant nothing to him. She noticed that he was careful not to touch her, even casually, as though he didn't quite trust himself.

There were times when she struggled not to give in to the impulse, when he was earnestly involved in explaining something to her, to push his hair off his forehead...or touch his cheek, or trace his lips with her finger.

Ian had unwittingly triggered a new awareness in her of her own sensual nature.

Ian pulled up a chair and sat down across the desk from her. "I've had an idea."

Jenna forced herself to concentrate on what he was saying instead of the shape of his jaw and the dimple in his chin. In the past month he had come up with several ideas about places of interest they could explore. This must be about another place he'd remembered.

"What is your idea?" she replied, amused at his show of enthusiasm.

"For another book."

She straightened. "Really?" She'd been working

on her résumé this past week in anticipation of the day when he no longer needed her. What if she didn't have to leave so soon?

"Yes. I woke up in the middle of the night with this story line running through my head. Whole scenes, with characters and everything."

She'd never seen him so animated. "Well. That's exciting."

"So I wish to formally hire you to help me with this new venture."

She laughed. "I thought you planned to return to full-time duty as soon as the manuscript goes in the mail."

"I know. I'm going to call Todd today and arrange a meeting with him. I need to set up a schedule of sorts to see if I will have time for both my writing and my career."

"That makes sense."

"To mark the conclusion of our first project, I suggest that you take a week or so off. You've more than earned a paid holiday. Explore the Highlands, visit historical sites, enjoy yourself. You deserve the time off."

When he mentioned time off, she'd jumped to the conclusion they would be going somewhere together. What nonsense. He had never implied that he wished their relationship to move beyond their working agreement.

"You're absolutely right," she said with conviction. "I could use a change," *and some space,* she added to herself. Perhaps being away from him for a while would cause her strong reaction to him to subside.

"I've been a slave driver, I know."

Briskly she said, "Let me finish these pages and we can talk about when I can get away."

A few hours later Ian returned to her office. "I talked to Todd just now and he told me to meet him on Thursday. Why don't you leave around the same time?"

"All right."

"Since I'll be in London, anyway, I thought I would take the manuscript with me and give it to Craig. That way you won't have to concern yourself with mailing it."

"Makes sense." She watched him closely as she said, "You'll know after the meeting when you'll be returning to London, won't you?"

"Or I may discuss being transferred to the northern region."

"I hope everything works out for you," she said calmly and picked up the pages he'd brought in to her. "Thanks for the update…and for the time off."

She watched him as he left the room. Would he decide to postpone working on his new idea once he returned to his job? There was no way for her to know.

Ian already missed Jenna and he'd been gone from the castle no more than a few hours. His flight to London had been uneventful and he'd spent the time thinking about how she had come into his life and created such a change in his routine and his thinking.

He'd been careful to keep a polite distance from her since the night they'd shared that passionate kiss. He only had so much willpower and he knew touching her would be a careless test of his control.

During these past weeks, he'd been reevaluating his life and priorities and he'd discovered that having her in his life was important to him. Not as his secretary so much as his friend, the person he turned to when he needed to talk something out. He didn't want to destroy that friendship by taking her to bed, or even just trying to get her into bed.

Once he arrived in London, Ian went directly to headquarters. He was early for his appointment.

When he walked into the office, the five-member staff greeted him with pleased surprise. Their greetings and concern for his health caught him off guard.

He was embarrassed. Some of them had worked there for as long as he had and yet he could remember only one name out of the group. Since he had the time, Ian paused to chat with them, asking how things had been going for them while he'd been gone. As a result he heard a thumbnail sketch from each of them. Their open, friendly responses to his polite questions touched him.

When it was time to keep his appointment with

Todd, he shook hands all around and thanked them for their concern.

Todd's assistant smiled when she saw him. "Go on in. He's expecting you."

When Ian stepped into the office Todd rose and walked around his desk. He held out his hand. "Ian! You're looking great, I must say. Glad you were able to meet with me."

Ian shook his hand. "I'm glad to be here. Telephone conversations are an inadequate way of communicating, in my opinion."

Todd chuckled and motioned to one of the chairs in front of his desk. "Have a seat. Would you like something to drink?"

"No, I'm fine. Thanks."

"Tell me how you're doing," Todd said, walking around the desk to his chair. "I know you've kept me up to date on your progress, but I'm talking about today. How are you feeling?"

"Other than the fact that my leg has become an accurate indicator of any weather change, I'm recovered. I continue to exercise to ensure its continued flexibility and I've returned to my regular workout."

Todd nodded. "You feel you're ready to come back, then."

"Yes."

Todd leaned back in his chair and studied him in silence. Finally, he said, "You want to continue in the field, I take it."

"Yes." Todd knew all of this. Ian wondered why he was going over the information again.

"How's the book coming?"

"I finished it."

"Good for you. What do you intend to do with it?"

"I'm giving it to Craig. He told me he would read it to see whether or not he thinks his father might be interested in looking at it."

"Yes, Craig would know, wouldn't he, having been brought up in a family of publishers. If Benson Publishing wants it, you'll be out there with the big guns. I couldn't be happier for you."

"Nothing's happened yet. Craig may find it embarrassingly amateurish. Let's wait to hear the verdict before we celebrate."

Todd nodded and said, "What would you think about a new assignment? With your skills we could certainly use someone to analyze and evaluate the intelligence information we gather. I think you'd make an excellent head of the group, training the younger ones to recognize when a seemingly innocuous piece of information can be vital."

"You're talking about a desk job."

"That's one of your options, yes."

"I prefer being out in the field, although I appreciate the promotion you're offering me. I've been wondering if there might be an opening for me in the northern district. I'd enjoy being stationed closer to home."

Todd smiled. "You've grown some deep roots while you've been recuperating in Scotland, have you?"

"Oh, the roots have always been there. Let's just say I've been nurturing them."

"If you're sure you don't want to take the position I'm offering, I'll talk to some people, check for any vacancies and get back with you. All right?"

"Thanks, Todd. I appreciate it."

Todd stood and Ian knew the meeting was concluded. He shook hands once again and said, "Thank you for taking the time to see me."

"My pleasure. I have to say that I've never seen you look so rested and relaxed. The time off has been good for you, I think."

"I would have preferred a forced vacation rather than using the time in recovery."

"You were damn lucky and you know it."

"Yes."

"We'll keep in touch," Todd said, and Ian left the office.

He had the strongest urge to call Jenna and tell her about the meeting even though it would do no good. She had, no doubt, left by now. He had no reason to hurry back to Scotland. He might spend the weekend here and look up some of the people he'd worked with, catch up on their news.

Jenna spent a week exploring some of the islands. She spent three nights on the Isle of Skye, one night on Mull and a day on Iona. Last night she had stayed in Oban. This morning she decided to drive to Inverness for the last two days of her holiday. She had stretched the week to include both weekends and felt that she was ready to return to her job in a different frame of mind.

She'd made use of the time to herself and had made several important decisions. She would spend less time with Ian when she returned. To make the change less obvious, she would spend more time in her room, doing crafts or needlework.

Otherwise she was going to be devastated when Ian returned to London permanently. She'd concluded that what she'd been thinking of as a harmless infatuation had become much more than that. Ian had begun to fill a void in her life. Living in such close proximity had drawn them together in a family setting. She hadn't felt a part of a family since her adoptive parents had died.

She'd grown used to sharing her daily life with another person, a man she was finding too easy to love. She still hoped to find Dumas, but her search was no longer in the forefront of her mind. Instead, most of her thoughts were about Ian.

And that scared her to death.

At least she now had an example of what she hoped to find in a man someday—one with integrity and intelligence, one who treated her as an equal, yet remained gentle with her.

How could she not love such a person?

She enjoyed the scenic drive along the string of lochs that led to Inverness. When she woke up the next morning she was blessed with sunshine, something she hadn't seen much of while she'd been at the coast.

Jenna spent her morning visiting nearby castles as well as the Culloden battlefield before returning to Inverness. She'd chosen the afternoon to do some much-needed shopping.

By midafternoon she had her hands filled with bags and decided she needed a break and a chance to get off her feet. She was looking for a place to have tea when she spotted a bookstore…her weakness. She couldn't resist going inside. Perhaps some day Ian's novel would be prominently displayed there. She could take pride in the fact that she had been a part of the process.

Jenna browsed the store and eventually plucked a new novel by one of her favorite authors off the shelf. She read the back cover blurb and knew she would enjoy it. When she turned to take it to the register she heard a woman's voice from behind her say, "Fiona! My, but you're looking fit. You've lightened the color of your hair, I see."

Jenna idly glanced around to see who had spoken and discovered the woman looking at her. Jenna stared at her. She'd never seen the woman. This must be a case of mistaken identity.

"I'm sorry, but I'm afraid—"

"Oh!" the woman exclaimed, blushing. "I'm so

sorry. I could have sworn you were Fiona Mac-Donald. You look just like her, but when you spoke, I realized the accent was wrong.''

''I'm from Australia.''

The woman continued to stare at Jenna in wonder. ''It's almost eerie, the way the two of you resemble each other. Now that I look closer, though, I see that your eyes are blue. Fiona has beautiful green eyes and striking red hair. Other than that, I swear the two of you could pass for twins!''

Jenna couldn't believe it. After all this time in Scotland, had she accidentally encountered someone who might have some information to help her find some relatives? Wouldn't it be wonderful, she thought, in a surge of excitement, if this Fiona could be kin to her?

She held out her hand. ''I'm Jenna Craddock. What you've said sounds wonderful to me—that is, that I should remind you of someone here in Scotland. You see, I've been hoping to find information about my family since I moved here this past spring.''

The woman took her hand. ''Emily. Emily Gillis,'' she replied.

''I have so many questions to ask you about your friend. Do you have a few moments?''

Emily smiled. ''My, you are excited, aren't you? Why don't we find a nice place for tea and we'll see if I can be any help.''

"Actually, I was looking for a place when I saw the bookstore."

"I know just the place. Follow me," Emily said.

Jenna looked at the forgotten book in her hand and replaced it on the shelf. She followed Emily out of the bookstore. "Do you live here in Inverness?" she asked.

Emily nodded. "George and I moved here almost three years ago now. Before that we lived in a little village called Craigmor. That's where I knew Fiona. Ah, here's the bakery I had in mind. Their scones melt in your mouth. Let's go find a table."

Jenna willingly accompanied Emily inside the aromatic shop. Thankfully the place wasn't crowded, since there were only four tables arranged along one wall. Emily told her to wait there and she would order their tea and scones.

Once seated, Emily said, "It's such a shame about Fiona, really."

Jenna's heart sank. "What's wrong with her?"

"Oh, not with her. We had just moved away when I heard that her parents—he was one of the local doctors—were killed while they were in Ireland on holiday. I don't recall the details. I wrote Fiona, sending my condolences. When she answered she said she was leaving Craigmor because of the memories and I'm afraid I lost track of her after that."

"Oh." Jenna's enthusiasm waned. "I had hoped to get to meet her. There may be no connection between us. Then again, she might know someone who could guide me in locating my real parents. I'm adopted, you see.''

''You don't say? Do you know your parents' names?''

''I'm afraid not. I have very little to go on, actually.''

''Well. It's a shame Dr. MacDonald is no longer alive. He might have heard of an arranged adoption from some of his colleagues. Of course there are those who wouldn't be too happy to have their past suddenly brought before them,'' she said, leaning closer and lowering her voice, ''if you know what I mean.''

''Of course. I'm not at all sure what I would do if I discovered their names. I doubt I'd contact them directly. But at least I'd be able to look up records and learn something about my background.'' She took a sip of her tea and reminded herself once again that the odds were formidable against her finding kin.

''Well, I could see about contacting her, wherever she might have moved. We have mutual friends who would probably know how I can find her.'' Emily smiled at Jenna. ''Where do you live, my dear?''

''I'm presently living and working at Durham Castle.''

''Really. As I recall, Durham is fairly close to Stirling, isn't it?''

''That's right.''

"You know, Craigmor is little more than an hour's drive north of Stirling. Wouldn't it be something if the two of you are related in some way? Distant cousins, perhaps. I would swear on a stack of Bibles that you have some common ancestor, for you to look so much alike."

"I'll admit I'm eager to find out."

Emily glanced at her watch. "I've enjoyed chatting with you but I need to get back home. George gets restless when I don't have his tea ready on time." They both stood. "Why don't you give me your address and a phone number where you can be reached. I'll see what I can find out for you and give you a ring in the next week or so."

Jenna wanted to hug the woman. Instead, she jotted down the requested information and handed it to Emily. "I really thank you for following up on this for me."

They parted in front of the bakery with a friendly wave and Jenna returned to her hotel.

Fiona. She wondered what information, if any, the woman might have that would help Jenna in her search? Jenna had neglected to ask how old Fiona was. Emily appeared to be in her mid- to late forties. Maybe Fiona was Emily's age. Wouldn't it be something if Fiona turned out to be her mother? She was jumping to conclusions. Anyway, as Emily said, few people would want to be confronted with a child they'd given up for adoption. If Jenna was able to find out names, she would allow that to be enough information for her.

What if Emily gave Fiona her number and Fiona contacted her? What would Jenna say to her? How would she explain her interest? She could imagine the woman's reaction if Jenna were to say, "I've been told I look like you. Do you suppose we're related?"

Fiona would think she was loony. And with good cause.

Jenna left Inverness early the next morning, and the closer she came to Ian the more excited she became. She could hardly wait to see him and tell him her news. She was less eager to hear when he intended to return to duty.

Nevertheless, she had a slim lead on her original quest. She would need the distraction once she concluded her work for Ian.

Chapter Nine

As soon as Jenna arrived at the castle, she took her bags to her room, freshened up from her travel and went in search of Ian. She found Hazel instead.

"Welcome back!" Hazel said, wearing a big grin. "You're looking quite rested, I must say."

"I'm feeling rested despite my trek through the western Highlands. Such beautiful country."

"Let me get you some refreshments."

"Oh, thank you. Is Ian here?"

She hadn't lasted a full minute before she'd spoken the question uppermost in her mind.

"Oh, he's somewhere. I've never seen him so restless as he's been since he returned from London. A day hasn't passed that he hasn't waylaid me asking if I'd heard anything from you."

Oh, my, Jenna thought. Is it because he missed me or— "He must have some dictation he's anxious to see transcribed," she replied lightly.

"He never said. Let's get you something to eat. If he doesn't show up by the time you're finished, we'll sound an alarm," Hazel said, laughing.

Jenna could see how being summarily summoned might not improve his already prickly disposition. "Or maybe not," she replied.

She'd finished her second cup of tea when Hazel returned. "Cook says she saw him in the gardens not long ago. He's probably hobnobbing with the groundskeeper, a sure sign he's restless and bored."

Jenna deliberately took her time with her light meal. The last thing she wanted was to appear too eager to locate him.

When she stepped through the French doors of the library Jenna couldn't believe the change in the gardens. Everything seemed to have blossomed since she'd been gone.

She followed the path that led toward the groundskeeper's house, pausing from time to time to enjoy the aroma of a particular flower.

Jenna was cupping a rose and daintily sniffing it when Ian rounded a curve in the path and spotted her. Thank God she was here! he thought, picking up his pace. His pulse rate increased as though he'd been running while he strode toward her.

"Hello," he said when he was within speaking distance.

"Oh!" she said, turning abruptly. "There you are! I was coming to look…ouch!" A rose thorn had pricked her index finger. She put the finger in her mouth and the sight was so erotic he was immediately aroused. "I was looking for you," she finished saying while he desperately thought of every unappealing subject he could to discourage his body from making a fool of him.

"Really. When did you return?"

"About an hour ago. Hazel had no idea where you might be. I decided to fortify myself with food and drink before I ventured out on my hunt for the laird of the castle."

He couldn't get enough of staring at her, memorizing the way her eyes crinkled at the corners and the dimple in her cheek flirted when she smiled. Or the way the sunlight caught the gold and red strands of her hair, burnishing them as though her hair projected its own light.

Ian stuffed his hands in his pockets before he broke his own rule about not touching her. He contented himself with the pleasurable knowledge that she was back here…where she belonged.

They spoke at the same time. "You'll never believe what's happened." Then stopped.

"Tell me," he said, strolling to a small bench in front of a flowing fountain. Wordlessly he motioned for her to take a seat, while he contented himself with bracing his foot along the ledge of the stonework surrounding the fountain.

"Oh, no. You first. Tell me about the meeting with Todd. When do you return to work?"

So much had happened since that meeting that he'd actually forgotten his original purpose for going to London. "Oh, well, he said he'd let me know."

"Oh. Then what is your big news?"

"By some miracle that I refuse to question, Craig handed off my manuscript to one of the Benson editors without telling me. I received a call from the publisher's office this morning asking me to return to London to discuss the manuscript, which is a favorable sign, I must say. I'm to attend some kind of cocktail affair on Wednesday night."

"Oh, Ian! I'm so pleased for you."

The warmth in his chest expanded when he saw her pleasure at his announcement. "You're going, too, of course," he added.

"Me? There's no reason for me to go, Ian. They want to meet the author, not the transcriber."

He straightened and sat next to her, throwing all his rules out the window. He took her hand and carefully massaged each knuckle. "I understand that accompanying me to social functions isn't part of your job description, but, please…take pity on me. You know how I hate attending those things."

"Yes, I do recall you mentioning it once or twice. Your mother will be pleased to hear you're willing to attend."

"All right, so you think this is a joke, do you?"

Sitting this close, he could lose himself in the blue depths of her entrancing eyes. "I'm to meet some of the staff that would be working on my book if they decide to buy. I'll be absolutely miserable in a room with not a single person I know." He brought her hand to his mouth and brushed his lips across it. "I need you, Jenna. I really do."

He might be overplaying his hand a little, but the more he thought about her going with him, the better he liked the idea. His reason for asking was that he'd already done without her for almost two weeks. He didn't want to go off and leave her now.

"Please?" he asked hopefully.

"You're incorrigible."

He smiled, sensing her acquiescence. "I do handle the role quite well, don't I?"

"Of being incorrigible?"

"As well as arrogant and decidedly opinionated. So. Will you go? I really don't want to face those people alone. I have no problem discussing the manuscript with them and I'm quite pleased they're considering it. It's having to stand around making inane conversation with people that makes me shudder."

She shook her head sadly. "You poor dear. All right. I'll go along to protect you from all the monsters and predators."

"Monsters and predators I can handle. They're easy compared to something like this!" He grinned at her, pleased to have gotten his own way.

"When do we need to leave?"

"Our flight is booked for early Wednesday morning. We'll attend the party that night, I'll meet with someone at the publisher's the next morning and we fly out that afternoon. Two days. That's all."

"Mmm. *Our* flight is booked?"

Oops. "If you hadn't wanted to go, I would have canceled yours. It made sense to book them together, just in case."

Her lips twitched, thank goodness, which meant she wasn't angry with him. "I see."

"A car will pick us up here and take us to the airport. We'll need to be ready to leave by five. Sorry it's so early."

"I don't mind, although I wish I'd known about this yesterday while I was shopping in Inverness. I'm afraid I have nothing appropriate to wear to such a gathering," she said, smiling ruefully.

"Go shopping tomorrow. I'll pay for it, since it's part of your job."

She pulled her hand away and he knew that somehow he'd offended her. "I have quite enough money to pay for my own clothes, but thank you for the offer."

"We can drive to Edinburgh, if you like. We'll make a day of it."

"I can't believe you, of all people, would consider following me around while I shop." She reached for his forehead. "Are you certain you're not coming down with something?" She realized what she'd done and hastily dropped her hand.

"I suppose I've missed you while you were away." Suppose? There's an understatement, he thought. "All right, you can shop while I run some errands of my own. We can have lunch, maybe do some sightseeing and come home. Will that suit?"

As though she'd only heard one statement, she said, "Ah, so you missed me. Now that's a surprise...unless you needed some typing done."

"You wound me. I'm not so self-absorbed as all of that, I hope. As a matter of fact, I've gotten in the habit mornings of watching you here in the gardens. You draw so much pleasure from such simple things. You seem to notice everything—the clouds, the flowers... I've seen you study a leaf with rapt absorption. I've never met anyone quite like you." He looked away, afraid he'd revealed too much.

"I learned a long time ago to appreciate what I had—which wasn't all that much when I was a child—rather than waste my time pining for things I don't have," she replied. Except for family, she reminded herself. She hadn't been able to halt the yearning to find family she could call her own.

As though aware of her troubling thoughts, he said, "Now it's your turn. Tell me what happened while you were away."

"Nothing so earthshaking as your news, I assure you. A woman in one of the bookstores in Inverness mistook me for someone else. When we began to talk, she said I looked enough like her friend to be her twin."

Ian felt chilled by the news. "You think you've found a relative?" Would she leave if she did? Would she prefer to spend time with others rather than to continue living there?

"Nothing so concrete, I'm afraid. In fact, the woman wasn't certain where her friend lives now. She said if she learned anything, though, she'd give me a ring."

Ian released the breath he'd been holding. Of course he wanted Jenna to find family, if that's what she wanted. There was no reason for him to feel so threatened by the idea. So why did he? She had no idea how he felt about her. For that matter, he wasn't certain himself.

"I've been working on the new story while you were away," he said. "You have a couple of tapes waiting for you but since today is your day off, I forbid you from entering your office until after we return from Edinburgh."

"If we're going to be gone tomorrow, I believe that would constitute my day off. Besides, I didn't get home today until almost three." She rose and took a deep breath. "I love the mingled scent of flowers here. You are so fortunate to have your own Garden of Eden."

Ian watched her walk away, her step jaunty and her shoulders back. Jenna was an independent woman who needed no one.

He'd always thought the same about himself. Until now.

The next morning Jenna stood in the entrance hall, waiting for Ian to appear.

She looked around her and idly wondered if she would have the opportunity while she was here to explore the entire castle without getting hopelessly lost, never to be heard of again. The thought amused her.

"Now there's a wicked grin if I ever saw one," Ian commented, joining her. "Care to share?"

"I was just thinking about how easy it is to get lost here. I suppose when the place was built that was considered a good defense. First the enemy would have to find you. Despite the fact that I've been in only a small portion of the castle I still get turned around from time to time."

They went out to his car. Once on their way to Edinburgh, Ian said, "As a child, after listening to several Grimm fairy tales, I once left a trail of bread crumbs when I decided to explore the older part of the house, until Cook—not Megan but an earlier one—scolded me for swiping a freshly baked loaf and encouraging mice. Never did that again."

"I'd contemplated getting a string if I had the courage to explore, but I'd have to buy so much I doubt I'd have a place to store it afterward." They smiled at each other.

The day turned into something magical. She'd never seen Ian so lighthearted. Of course he would be, knowing there was a good chance he'd sold his manuscript to the first publisher who read it. How often did that happen?

As he promised, Ian dropped her off at one of the large department stores once they arrived in Edinburgh. They arranged to meet for lunch at a certain time and place, so that Jenna had more than enough time to shop for a dress.

She wasn't certain what she was looking for, exactly. But she knew she wanted something that would cause Ian to see her as a woman and not just a stenographer.

By the time they returned home, she felt the day had been a success. Ian had taken on the role of tour guide. They'd visited both Holyrood and Edinburgh castles and she'd been surprised at how knowledgeable Ian was. She went to sleep that night knowing she would never forget the memories they'd made that day.

When they landed in London on Wednesday morning, a chauffeur met them. He held a placard with Ian's name on it. The publisher had not only sent a car for them, he had arranged for their accommodations for the night. The closer they got to London, the more nervous Jenna became about the sleeping arrangements. Had Ian explained that she was his secretary and not his girlfriend?

She could only hope. Otherwise, the situation could become horribly embarrassing. Her embarrassment was of a different sort once they arrived at the hotel and she and Ian were shown to a luxury suite. Jenna had never stayed in a luxury hotel before. For that matter, she'd stayed in very few hotels during her life, period. A surprisingly large sitting room separated the two bedrooms. She hoped her amazement didn't make her appear to be a complete ninny. She turned in a slow circle, trying to see everything at once.

She watched Ian tip the bellman and close the door behind him.

"So." He glanced around. "Here we are. Choose whichever bedroom you prefer." He walked to the window without glancing at her and stared out. "Good view. Not that we'll be here all that much to enjoy it."

Jenna followed him to the window and stood beside him. "London is really quite lovely, isn't it?"

He glanced at her. "Haven't you been here before?"

"Technically, yes. However, I didn't see much of it. Most of my time was spent shuttling between the airport and the car rental place."

"Would you like to see a few things today? At least visit the Tower of London, perhaps Westminster Abbey?"

"I'd like that if we aren't gone too long. I'll need to rest before the party tonight or I'll be asleep on my feet by nine o'clock."

"I think we can handle that." He held out his hand. "Come on. Let's go pretend to be tourists."

"Pretend! I'll have you know I'm a bona fide tourist."

He kept her hand in his in a protective grip for most of the day.

Chapter Ten

That evening, Ian glanced at his watch while he restlessly paced the sitting room floor. The car was to pick them up in twenty minutes. Maybe he'd have a drink to steady his nerves. He went to the wet bar and found an aged Scotch whiskey that would do nicely.

He wondered if Jenna had any idea how serious he'd been about needing her to accompany him tonight? He wasn't at all certain he would have shown up, otherwise, which would not have made the best impression on the publisher to whom he hoped to sell his manuscript.

Sipping his whiskey, he wandered to the window and looked out at the scene below him. With any luck he could show up at the party, acknowledge introductions and leave soon afterward.

"I'm sorry to keep you waiting."

"We have plenty of time," he said, turning toward her. As soon as he saw her, Ian forgot what he was going to say.

She wore a black, sleeveless dress that clung to her body, throwing her small waist and slim hips into bold relief. The V-neck displayed a fair amount of cleavage. From his vantage point he saw the curve of her breasts quite clearly, making him immediately decide to have another drink.

She walked toward him, calling attention to the short hem that revealed her slender legs. The high-heeled shoes she wore arched her foot, drawing attention to her delicate ankles.

In other words, she would not only stop traffic dressed that way, she'd have every man who saw her drooling down the front of his shirt, starting with him.

"Ah, so this is the dress you found," he said after clearing his throat.

She grinned. "Like it?" she asked, turning slowly to show all sides.

The back plunged farther than the front, revealing the delicate bones of her spine. There was no way in hell she could be wearing a bra.

Ian swallowed, suddenly feeling inordinately territorial. He had no words that could express what he was feeling. He just knew that he was in big trouble.

"Would you like to join me in a drink?" he asked, holding his glass up. "I'm afraid I started without you."

Jenna grinned and walked toward him. "My, don't you look grand," she said. "You look quite austere in your black suit. I expected to see you wearing kilts."

"Not tonight." He went to the bar and lifted his brow in a question.

"White wine, please."

"Waiting to go out for the evening seems quite domestic, doesn't it?" he said, handing her a glass.

Only when she flushed did he realize that she might misinterpret his comment.

"Sorry," he said abruptly. "That was my attempt at being witty. Perhaps I'll remain silent at the party rather than open my mouth and say the wrong thing."

Jenna widened her eyes in feigned horror. "What? And return to your usual grouchy self?" she teased. "Oh, please. Be witty, by all means."

He grinned and grabbed his chest. "A direct hit. So I'm grouchy, am I? How deflating. I believe I'm crushed."

"There, that was quite a witty thing to say, since anyone who knows you is aware you couldn't care less what anyone thinks of you."

He took her free hand and brought it to his mouth. "I thought I was doing much better in the grouchy department lately," he murmured, brushing his lips across her knuckles.

She smiled, betraying a hint of vulnerability he'd never seen in her. She appeared to be so self-possessed as a general rule.

"You've improved immensely," she replied lightly. "I actually heard you laugh on Monday." She half closed her eyes and tapped her foot thoughtfully. "Hazel and I thought it was one of the gardeners at first. I believe we both marked the event on our calendars."

"All right. You win. Our car should be here by now, thank God, before we continue to air a list of all my shortcomings." Ian reluctantly released her hand when she stepped away from him. He watched as she picked up her thin wrap from the back of the sofa.

Leaving the room together gave him an odd sense of pleasure. This was the closest thing to a date he'd had in too long a time. Despite having to attend a party, Ian intended to enjoy himself. Hopefully, Jenna would forget, for tonight at least, that he was her boss. He much preferred that she see him as a man with whom she wanted to spend time.

Jenna kept her eyes on the lift at the end of the hall so that she wouldn't continue to gape at Ian like some lovelorn teen. When she'd first seen him looking out the window with one hand in his pocket, the other casually holding a drink, her first thought had been, *Oh, my gosh! James Bond!* The austere black suit and dazzling white shirt emphasized his broad shoulders and lean hips.

They walked through the lobby of the hotel with her hand resting on his arm. Jenna felt like Cinderella being escorted to the ball. *This is not the time to start fantasizing,* she reminded herself with a mental shake. Reality is too much like a fantasy to attempt to improve on it.

Their driver told them that the party was being held in the penthouse of what was obviously an expensive condominium, if the ornate lobby was any indication. She was so busy taking in everything around her that Jenna forgot about her nervousness. However, once inside the lift with Ian by her side, her heart picked up its pace as she braced herself for whatever would happen next.

He reached for her hand and held it firmly, as though he found her touch reassuring. Despite his insistence that parties terrified him, Ian had an aristocratic air that intimidated more often than not. He was a man who appeared to have no fears—unless you counted attending parties.

She ducked her head to hide her smile at the thought.

As soon as they stepped off the lift a wave of sound hit them, a combination of live music, high-pitched conversations and sudden shouts of laughter. Perhaps Ian had good reason to dread these gatherings!

''Ah, there you are, Ian,'' someone said after

breaking away from a group standing in front of double doors that opened to the suite. "I was wondering if you'd changed your mind about coming."

"Hello, Craig. I didn't expect to see you here tonight," Ian replied, relaxing slightly.

"Oh, I wasn't invited. I hit up the old man for a finder's fee on your book so I came to protect my investment." He looked at Jenna, his eyes widening. "Well, hello. I'm Craig Benson. And you are—"

"With me," Ian replied dryly, "so behave yourself. Jenna, this wolf in wolf's clothing is Craig Benson. I believe I've mentioned him once or twice."

Jenna wanted to laugh. Craig was being polite, she knew, but that didn't stop Ian from moving closer to her and dropping his arm around her shoulders. "This is Jenna Craddock."

"How do you do?" she asked, offering her hand. Instead of shaking it, Craig gracefully brought it to his lips and kissed it. "My pleasure, pretty lady." Jenna wondered if Ian saw the quick look Craig threw his way before he winked at her. Men, she thought. What was it about them that made them competitive about everything?

Craig was of medium height with dark hair and gray eyes. Although his smile was mischievous, his eyes told a different story. "I understand you and Ian work together," she said politely.

He glanced at Ian. "Let's just say we're in the same line of work."

He gave Ian a sober look and Jenna wondered

what, exactly, was their line of work? "Come with me," Craig said. "I'll introduce you to Dad and after that, I'll give you a running commentary on who's here and who you need to meet."

A small combo played at one end of the large living room. An area had been cleared for dancing. Knots of people decorated the room with everyone seemingly talking at once.

In an alcove off the main room, a heavily laden buffet table enticed the crowd.

Ian still had his arm around her shoulders and she was grateful for his guidance through the chattering groups of people. Craig came to a stop next to a small group by the giant fireplace and said, "Here he is," quietly to his father.

Alfred Lloyd Benson turned and looked at them. Benson was a tall, rather thin and slightly stoop-shouldered man in his fifties who exuded an abundance of energy.

"Ah, yes. Ian MacGowan, is it?" he boomed. "Glad you could make it."

"Thank you for inviting us," Ian responded smoothly. "May I introduce you to Jenna Craddock, who thought she should come along to keep me in line."

His words were so unexpected, and his demeanor so serious, that Jenna was caught off balance. Her face flamed.

"Pleased to meet you, young lady," Benson said.

He turned to Ian. "We have a meeting in the morning, is that right?"

"Yes, sir. At ten."

"Good, good. Well, Craig will show you around and introduce you to people. Help yourself to the buffet and the bar. I look forward to talking with you."

Ian glanced at Jenna and she knew exactly what he was thinking—they could leave now. She smiled serenely and looked at Craig. "Let's start with that group over there," he said with a nod. "Word about your manuscript has already spread. Just between you and me, they're eager to get their hands on it. I read no more than fifty pages and knew you have a winner there."

Jenna felt Ian relax for the first time since they'd arrived. Well, why not? Any new author—or an experienced one, for that matter—would want to hear he'd written a good book.

She sympathized with Ian, though. The purpose of their attending tonight's gathering had been served as far as Ian was concerned. The rest of their time would be spent going through the social maneuvering of polite society.

Craig introduced them to a great many people who seemed delighted to meet Ian, while a few of the women unobtrusively checked to see if they wore wedding rings. Amused, but not surprised by Ian's abrupt way of handling new acquaintances,

Jenna remained silent and listened to the swirl of conversation around them.

Eventually, Jenna became separated from Ian, which was just as well. She really needed to sit. Her feet were reminding her that she wasn't used to wearing such high heels for an extended period of time. She was grateful to find a quiet corner where she could observe her surroundings.

"Would you like a drink?"

She glanced up and saw a waiter with several flutes of champagne on a tray. "Thank you," she said, accepting a glass and sipping from it as the waiter continued on his rounds.

"You look abandoned here all alone. Would you like some company?" someone said a few minutes later. She looked up to see a distinguished gentleman with silver hair smiling at her.

"I haven't been abandoned, but I would enjoy your company," she replied. There was something about him that brought Basil Fitzgerald to mind. She smiled. "I'm Jenna Craddock," she added.

He sat in the chair next to hers. "Anthony Teasdale, but everyone calls me Tony. Alfred and I met at Eton years ago and have remained close friends ever since. What brings you here this evening?"

"I'm with Sir Ian MacGowan." She nodded to where Ian stood with several people—mostly women, she idly noted—who all appeared to be talking at the same time.

She returned her gaze to Tony, and the two of them began to chat.

* * *

Ian looked around, wondering where Jenna had gone. He'd been very much aware when she'd slipped away but didn't comment. He'd been too busy acknowledging introductions. He hoped no one expected him to remember half the names he'd heard tonight. Another mark against him in his mother's book. She'd pointed out that if he halfway paid attention instead of looking for the nearest exit, he would have no trouble recalling the names of people he met.

Eventually he spotted Jenna seated near the French doors that opened onto the terrace. She was listening with rapt attention to a man old enough to be her grandfather.

Ian frowned. He needed to keep an eye on her. After all, he was responsible for her being there. Since neither of them knew the other guests, it was only sensible that he stay close by. He noted that more than one gentleman was close to salivating into his drink when he first spotted her. Interestingly enough, Jenna appeared oblivious to those watching her and vying for her attention. Didn't she wonder why there was so much traffic out to the terrace and back? A couple of the men were undressing her with their eyes.

It was time for him to let others know that Jenna was with him. He almost wished that Craig had stayed with her. He could handle Craig. Hell. If he had to, he could handle all of them, although he was a trifle outnumbered tonight.

Ian was halfway across the living room when he heard a woman's voice say, "Ah, there you are, Ian."

He turned and saw a tall brunette with predatory eyes bearing down on him. He looked at her with suspicion. Who the hell was this?

She slid her arm inside his so that her breast pressed against him. "I wanted to introduce myself," she said in a throaty voice.

He lifted his brow and waited.

"I'm Laurie Townsend," she said, smiling. "I'll be your editor for that marvelous manuscript you wrote. I could *not* put it down until I'd finished it, despite a desk piled high with urgent matters. You made everything sound so frightfully real. I don't know how you were able to turn out such an exciting first novel. I fully expect it to make the bestsellers' list soon after it's released." When he made no comment, she added, "You and I will be working closely in the next few months in order to make necessary changes." Her brilliant smile added a silent message, as well. "I'm looking forward to the task."

"Thank you," he replied, looking over at Jenna. Two more men were now seated around her. She radiated delight over whatever one of them was saying. When he finished, the group laughed heartily, including Jenna. She made a comment that garnered another round of laughter. He wished to hell he could hear past the noise in the room.

He replaced his empty glass with a full one from a passing waiter, taking a healthy swallow. He didn't realize he was still staring at Jenna until Laurie spoke.

"Your date is quite lovely. Have you known her long?" Laurie asked, following his gaze.

"Long enough, I should think." Yes. They'd gotten to know each other quite well, he thought. She'd put up with his abrupt manner at a time when he'd been unreasonably difficult with everyone. She deserved a golden tiara for that, he was certain.

He continued to keep his eye on her, fully aware that he was keeping a tight grip on his control. Because what he would like to do at the moment was to walk over there, brush every hovering male away from her, throw her over his shoulder and take her to bed.

For at least a week.

Maybe longer.

Who said he wasn't civilized? He'd merely thought those things, not acted upon them.

Yet.

He was an idiot.

"Long enough for what?" Laurie purred close to his ear, her black eyes looking up at him through her lowered lashes.

"I beg your pardon?"

"You said you've known her long enough."

He carefully removed her hand from his arm. "If you'll excuse me," he murmured and walked away. That was going to be his editor? God help him. If his instincts were as well honed as he thought, he'd be a fool to be anywhere alone with the woman. She'd probably trip him and fall under him before he knew what had happened.

He heard Jenna's voice as he neared the group, answering one of the men's questions about Australia.

With muttered apologies Ian made his way to her side, half sitting on the arm of her chair in what he hoped her audience would consider a possessive pose. He smiled at her and she reached for his hand, holding it tightly, smiling all the while.

Ah, she hadn't been prepared for all this attention, either.

"Would you like to join me?" he asked smoothly. "The buffet table has been beckoning since we arrived."

Her glance made his heart quiver. "Thank you," she replied, rising. Before walking away with him, she told the group around her that she had enjoyed their conversation.

Once they were away from the group, she added, "I appreciate the rescue."

"Don't mention it. I was serious about the buffet. Why don't we find something to eat and slip away after that? I believe I've done my duty here, and the food looks delicious.'' They each filled a plate and found a small table where they could set their drinks. ''I've never understood the preference for eating standing while juggling your glass, have you?'' he asked.

''Perhaps they don't want us to linger over our food. If we were at a banquet, we'd be spending all evening eating with very little chatting.''

He swallowed a bit of food and said, ''Sounds good to me,'' with heartfelt sincerity.

She laughed. ''You seemed quite entranced with the black-haired woman? A friend of yours?''

''Never saw her before in my life.'' He took another bite of food.

''Really? The two of you seemed cozy,'' Jenna said with the tiniest edge to her voice.

Suddenly Ian was enjoying himself…and why not? Good food, good drinks and a woman he couldn't stop thinking about was showing signs of jealousy.

What more could a man ask for?

''Do you want anything more from the buffet?'' he asked when they'd finished the food on their plates.

She shook her head. ''No, thank you.''

''Then I believe we've done our duty. Are you ready to leave?''

''My feet are definitely saying yes,'' she replied, smiling in a way that caused him to tremble. That dimple was definitely flirting with him.

"We'll find Benson and be on our way." He took her hand and led her into the next room.

"I've had a wonderful day in London, but I'm not sorry to see it come to an end," she said.

He stopped and looked at her. "Once we return to the hotel, I hope to convince you that the evening is still young."

Chapter Eleven

By the time they reached their suite, Ian felt like a callow schoolboy on his first date. His palms were sweaty and he had the horrifying thought that if he attempted to speak, his voice would crack.

He didn't know what had happened to him since Jenna had come into his life but it was damned uncomfortable. He was behaving as though he'd never been with a woman before, which was ludicrous. He'd been with enough women to handle himself with no problem.

He clutched the thought to himself like a life preserver.

Jenna walked into the room ahead of him, made a beeline for the sofa and sat, immediately slipping off her shoes and rubbing her arches. "Ahhh. That's better," she said, looking up at him with a mischievous grin.

Drawn to her warmth and beauty, Ian followed her to the sofa and sat next to her.

"Here, let me." He shifted her so that her feet were in his lap, took one of them in his hands and began to massage.

When he first touched her she looked startled, then a little dazed. Once he worked his thumbs into her delicate arch, she closed her eyes and sighed.

Except for the sound of their breathing, the room was silent. Eventually Jenna said, "I know the polite thing for me to do is to tell you that you really don't have to do this. However, I feel I should warn you that if you stop anytime soon, I might be forced to do you bodily harm." She settled into the sofa a little more, her skirt inching to just above her knees. "That feels marvelous."

He took her other foot and massaged the muscles in the same way as he had the first one.

Jenna closed her eyes and from all appearances was relaxed. However, touching her as he was, he could feel the tension in her, which she obviously wanted to hide from him.

Finally he stopped, letting his hands rest on her ankles.

She opened her eyes and looked at him. The only lamp lit in the room was on the table beside her. Abruptly he said what he was thinking.

"You look quite beautiful, you know, sitting there. The lamp gives your skin a glow very much like alabaster. I don't believe I've ever noticed that about you before. I can't imagine why."

She looked startled and shifted her feet. He clamped down on her ankles so she couldn't pull away. "Well. I, uh, thank you."

"There wasn't a man at the party tonight who didn't want to be the one who had brought you, or the one to take you home." He ran his thumb down her foot, circling back along her arch.

"I think that maybe we should call it a night, don't you?" she asked, her voice quavering slightly.

"Are you tired?"

She made a strangled sound before saying, "Aren't you?"

"I wouldn't mind stretching out on a bed to give my leg a rest," he mused.

"Oh. Yes, of course. Well, I'll just—" She waved her hand as though they both knew what she would just…do next.

He stood and held out his hand to her. She swung her legs to the floor and took his hand, her eyes wide.

"May I kiss you?" He sounded hoarse but he couldn't help that.

She stared at him, first into his eyes, then down to his lips. She swallowed and warm color flooded her cheeks. "I don't think that's too much to ask," she replied, and her trembling voice gave away her nervousness. "After all, it isn't as though we haven't kissed before." She moved hesitantly toward him and placed her hands on his chest. "Thank you for bringing me to London, Ian."

"You needn't thank me. It was all Benson's doing. But this has nothing to do with Benson." He lifted her so that her face was even with his, his arms holding her beneath her hips. She leaned in to him and gently kissed him, but it was far from enough. With a groan he slid one arm up her back and around her shoulders, taking over the kiss.

"Oh, Ian," she whispered after several long minutes that had steamed up the room.

"I can't believe I'm saying this," he replied, his voice shaking, "but I want to make love to you...rather desperately, actually."

The scene was like so many of Jenna's dreams that she expected to wake up at any moment. *Please don't wake up now!* She gazed into his eyes and said, "I thought you'd *never* ask!"

He gave a relieved laugh and turned in a circle with her pressed tightly against him before he strode into her bedroom. A soft light revealed that her bedcovers had been turned back. He let her slide down his long length until her feet touched the floor, then stepped back to look at her.

"There's really not much to that dress, is there?" he said with a grin and slid the zipper down. The dress slipped forward off her shoulders before falling to the floor, leaving her wearing nothing more than tiny briefs and thigh-high black stockings.

Frantic to get him undressed, Jenna pushed his coat off his shoulders and attacked his shirt, wishing he weren't wearing so many clothes.

Ian chuckled at her eagerness and said, "Let me remove the tie before you strangle me with it, okay?"

She should feel embarrassed at her lack of control... And what had happened to her modesty? She'd never been undressed in front of a man before.

Her eyes widened when she saw Ian remove a great deal more than his tie. He stood before her in all his male glory, fully aroused, wearing only his socks.

"Oh, my" was all she could say. Of course she knew about sex. She'd heard all about it at much too young an age. The idea had repulsed her at the time. But now? Now all she could do was stare at him in awe. Was it physically possible for them to...?

He shoved the covers out of the way and placed her on the bed before removing his socks and joining her. The look of concentration on his taut face and the searing heat of his eyes mesmerized her.

"You're magnificent, Jenna," he whispered, placing a kiss at her throat. She quivered, uncertain what to do next. He peeled her stockings off, tossing them to the floor, then ran his fingers beneath the satin and lace that made up her panties, slipping them off and tossing them, as well.

Ian brushed his lips along the crest of her breast, causing it to bead tightly before he pulled the tip into his mouth. His tongue was driving her crazy. She couldn't lie still. She shifted restlessly, her skin tingling everywhere he touched her.

And he seemed to be touching her everywhere—with his lips, his hands, his tongue. She felt hot and restless and impatiently ran her hands up and down his long, muscular back, pausing to caress his muscled derriere.

He rewarded her by kissing her so passionately she was afraid she would explode any moment into tiny pieces of pleasure.

"I have protection," he murmured, pulling away slightly and reaching for his pants. He quickly removed his billfold from his pants, took out the foil-covered disc and covered himself.

She hadn't given protection a thought! Not surprising, really. She wasn't sure she could *find* a sane thought at the moment.

He shifted and knelt between her knees. When he gently touched her with his fingers, she was embarrassingly damp. He didn't seem concerned in the least.

Unable to keep quiet any longer, Jenna said, "Are you sure—?"

"Honey, it's a little late to be asking me that now!"

"—that it will fit?"

He bit his bottom lip before he bent down and kissed her. Hard. "We'll do just fine."

She stiffened. There. Just as she'd always thought. She felt invaded. He was so large and— Oh. That was his finger slipping inside her, slowly stroking until she wanted to purr. Being invaded really wasn't such a bad idea after all, she thought, with the right person.

He brought her knees up, spreading them a little wider, and slowly pressed against her. "You're so small," he said, breathing harshly. "I don't want to hurt you."

She could feel herself stretching as he entered her, and she almost panicked, thinking that maybe he wouldn't fit. Then what would they do? With her feet flat on the bed, Jenna suddenly pushed her hips up tightly against his, embedding him deep inside her.

He froze and looked at her blankly. "Jenna?"

She stared at him, feeling engulfed by him. This is Ian, she reminded herself, and she'd wanted this for months.

"What?" she whispered.

"Why didn't you tell me?" He sounded almost angry.

She reached up and rubbed the frown lines from between his brows. "You look so ferocious when you frown."

"Don't change the subject," he said gruffly.

"All right. Be ferocious, I don't care." She raised her head to kiss him and he abruptly turned his head to the side. She sighed. Of course she knew what he was asking.

"Does it matter?" she finally asked, afraid that he was going to change his mind about this.

"Well, yes, as a matter of fact it does," he replied brusquely. "If you'd bothered to fill me in earlier, we wouldn't be here."

She wrapped her arms fiercely around him. "Then I'm glad you didn't know," she replied, planting tiny kisses on his face.

As though realizing there was no going back to the way things had been, Ian kissed her in a softer, gentler and yet still passionate way, not moving inside her. She was growing used to the fullness and slid her hips back from him, then closer.

"You're making it very difficult for me to concentrate on not hurting you, you know," he managed to say. "If I'd known this was your first time, I wouldn't have been so…so…" As though losing his train of thought, Ian began to move inside her.

Oh, my! That felt so…so… She couldn't think of the words. All she knew was that she didn't want him to stop.

When his rhythm increased she wrapped her legs around his thighs, and he moaned softly. She could feel herself tightening inside and without warning her body clenched, and then she was pulsating around him.

He cried out—holding her so tightly she could scarcely breathe. Then he collapsed against her, his head falling on her shoulder, before he rolled over onto his side next to her, his head on her pillow. His body glistened and his heart pounded so hard she could still feel its beat.

From experiencing the most intense sensations of pleasure she'd ever known, she went to stark fear at the realization that, in her ignorance, she had obviously done something dreadfully painful to him.

His cry hadn't sounded pleasured. Remembering the look on his face, she knew that she hadn't imagined his pain.

What had she done!

He lay so still…as though unable to move. If it wasn't for his heavy breathing she might think he had lapsed into unconsciousness. Jenna closed her eyes tightly, wondering what to do next.

Should she attempt to explain to him that she hadn't been able to control the spasms that took over her body? Would he care? How unfair that he gave her so much pleasure while she offered him nothing but pain.

No one had ever discussed that part of the sexual act. In fact, what she'd heard growing up was that it was the male who got all the fun out of the act, not the woman.

There must be something seriously wrong with her.

Jenna had no idea how long they lay in that position. She was afraid to move. She watched Ian closely, hoping he'd recover soon.

Eventually Ian sighed, inhaled deeply and raised his head.

"You're frowning," he said abruptly, propping himself on his elbow. Since he was wearing his ferocious scowl, this was like the pot calling the kettle black. "I hurt you, didn't I?" he asked, or more accurately, demanded to know. "Oh, Jenna, sweet one, I am so very, very sorry. You probably don't understand about this, but I haven't been with a woman for a long while and I lost control. You deserve so much more than that for your first time."

He stroked wisps of hair away from her face. "I promise to make it better for you next time, okay?"

"Better for *me?* It was unbelievably great for me." She eyed him uncertainly. "I thought I'd hurt you. Are you all right?"

He briefly closed his eyes. When he opened them his frown was gone...and his lips twitched. "Oh, yes. I'm quite all right." He sounded very polite, which she found a little disconcerting.

"What about your leg?

"What leg?" he repeated with a grin. "Believe me, at the moment I'm feeling no pain." He leaned closer and kissed her on the nose. "Did you really think you hurt me?"

She swallowed. "Yes. You looked as though you were in pain."

He burst into laughter. In fact, she'd never heard

him laugh with such delight. Too bad she wasn't in on the joke. When he grew quiet, he said, as though to himself, "How was I ever so fortunate to have you walk into my life, Ms. Jenna Craddock?"

She stroked his chin with her finger, following the contour of his rather stubborn jaw and pausing in the indentation in the middle of his chin. "Ms. Spradlin sent me," she replied honestly.

"Remind me to send her flowers as soon as we return home," he murmured, and began to make love to her all over again…another thing she'd been told couldn't happen.

Well, somebody certainly got their facts wrong, she thought, responding to him with more enthusiasm than skill.

She couldn't be happier with her discovery.

Jenna awoke some time during the night, startled to discover she was in bed with someone. Then she remembered. She was lying on her side tucked into Ian's curled body so that she felt the heat of his body from her shoulders to her toes.

She'd never slept nude before. There were many things that she had never done before tonight. Jenna wondered what they would say to each other in the morning. After all these months, she had experienced what it would be like to make love to Ian. It was much better than any of her fantasies.

The next time she opened her eyes, Ian was kissing and caressing her and she was on fire. She returned his kisses and caresses, which soon escalated into passionate lovemaking.

When Jenna awoke again, she sat up, blinking at the light coming in through the window. Glancing at her watch, she discovered it was almost eleven o'clock.

Eleven! She jumped out of bed. Ian had missed his appointment. He should have been— She saw a note on his pillow.

"Didn't have the heart to wake you. Sleep in. We have the room until three. I'll probably be back by noon."

Jenna had plenty of time to enjoy the large tub with the water jets before he was due to return. She noticed she had a few aches that were unfamiliar. Still nude, she paused in front of the mirrored wall by the tub and studied her image.

Did it show? she wondered. Was virginity something people could see in a person's face, recognizing when it was no longer there? Peering closely, all she saw was her tangled hair.

With a sudden grin, she winked at her image and whirled away to the counter to find her brush. While the hot water gushed into the tub, she brushed her hair and pulled it up into a knot at the top of her head.

Once the tub filled, she carefully stepped inside and sank into the warm depths. She'd never seen a tub this large before. It was nearly as wide as it was long. A person could have a swim party in this thing.

She turned on the jets and let the water bubble around her as she drifted into a restful state, her head resting on the side of the tub.

No doubt it was the noise of the jets that muffled Ian's return. The first she knew he was there was the unusual movement of the water splashing against her. She opened her eyes and saw him settling into the other end of the tub.

"Great idea. Glad you thought of it."

Sitting in a tub with him removed the idea she'd had of treating him the same as she always had—as her employer. There was something about his bare chest…and possibly that wicked smile…that caused her to think he wasn't thinking about being her employer at the moment.

Then he made his move.

They were late meeting their car for the airport that afternoon, which embarrassed Jenna as they crossed the lobby because she felt certain everyone who saw them knew exactly why they'd been delayed. She refused to look at their driver.

Once in the air, Jenna kept sneaking glances at Ian. The lines around his mouth were gone and he looked rested, which was surprising given how little sleep they'd had.

She hadn't remembered to ask him about his meeting with the publisher. Before she could bring up the subject, he caught her watching him and gave her a lazy smile. "Feel free to nap, if you'd like.

You can use my shoulder.'' As though her answer had already been given, he put his arm around her and pulled her closer, lifting the armrest that had been between them.

She thought about protesting but couldn't resist a few more hours of being close to him. She was almost asleep when she felt him brush his mouth against her forehead.

For the first time since she could remember, Jenna felt safe and very content.

Chapter Twelve

Ian and Jenna stopped to eat after they landed, so they arrived home late.

Ian placed their bags by the stairway and stretched.

"You were the one who should have slept on the plane," Jenna said, smiling. "How many hours of sleep did you get last night?"

He grinned. "Enough, obviously," he said with meaning.

"I highly recommend you as a pillow."

He started to say something, stopped and looked at her. "You know, I don't recall anyone before you who had the audacity to tease me."

"Then it's obvious your education is sadly lacking. I'll do my best to overlook it."

He grabbed her in a bear hug, kissing her as laughter bubbled between them. When he finally eased his grip, he said, "I suppose I shall get used to it."

She was startled when Hazel spoke from somewhere behind her.

"The trip was pleasant, I hope," Hazel said dryly, as though finding Jenna in Ian's arms was an ordinary happening. "Are you wanting something to eat before you're off to bed?"

Ian released Jenna slowly, as though reluctant to let her go. She immediately turned to face Hazel, knowing she was blushing.

"We stopped earlier," Ian answered. "But thank you for checking."

"Then I'm off to bed. I look forward to hearing how your trip went." She smiled at both of them and disappeared into the shadows of the hallway.

Ian brought Jenna's hand up to his lips and kissed it as he said, "You jumped when Hazel appeared, as though expecting to be banished immediately from the kingdom."

"Yes. Well. She startled me." Jenna glanced around to see if Hazel had left before saying, "Do you suppose she knows we slept together last night?"

"She might have her suspicions, I would say."

Jenna buried her face into his shirt. "I'll never be able to face her again."

"You needn't worry. I believe Hazel is aware that

such things happen between adults. I doubt she's all that surprised. Why does it bother you?''

"I feel guilty for seducing you, I suppose.''

"You must be joking!''

She leaned back into his arms. ''Surely you know I purchased that dress in hopes that it would entice you enough that you would want to make love to me.''

"Jenna…honey…it wouldn't have mattered if you'd worn a tent. I would have done any and everything I could to convince you to go to bed with me last night. I thought that was rather obvious.''

"Really?''

He shook his head and took her by the hand. ''I'll see what I can do to convince you,'' he said, and started up the stairs.

"Where are you going?''

He paused. ''To your room. Why?''

"You mean that you…that we…that…'' She came to a stumbling halt.

"That's absolutely right. You and me…we…are retiring to your room. Unless you'd prefer to spend the night in my quarters.''

"Oh, no!'' she said quickly. ''I, uh, thought that once we came back—''

"It's too late to pretend there's nothing between us, you know. I want to sleep with you. Whether we make love or not will be up to you.'' He continued up the stairs.

"You told me the first day I was here that you didn't want a personal relationship."

"I didn't, but you managed to convince me otherwise."

"Ian!" She halted abruptly at the top of the stairs. "I didn't do anything to encourage you."

As though tired of their slow progress, he picked her up and strode down the hallway to her room.

They were both breathless once they closed her door behind them. "That couldn't have been good for your leg."

"Believe me, my leg isn't my problem at the moment." He had them both undressed and into bed in little more than a minute.

Despite her protests, Jenna was as hungry for him as he appeared to be for her. She was damp and throbbing and he surged into her with little foreplay.

She didn't notice. Instead, she clung to him, urging him on so that the passion increased until they both exploded with almost painful climaxes.

Jenna couldn't move. She reminded herself that she needed to put on a sleep shirt. That was the last thing she remembered.

She stirred hours later when Ian slipped out of bed. She mumbled something and he said, "I'm going to my room in an effort to ease your embarrassment." His tone was light and teasing.

She squinted at the clock. It would be light soon. She snuggled into the covers warmed by his body and went back to sleep.

* * *

Three weeks later, Jenna awoke with a melody running through her head. She couldn't recall the name of the song but it was upbeat, which suited her mood quite well. She had never been so happy before and she reveled in the experience.

During the day Ian treated her politely and professionally. He spent the nights teaching her the many ways they could pleasure each other. Last night, in particular, was memorable. He'd massaged a creamy lotion over her body, taking particular care in all the creases and crevices. By the time he'd finished she was frantic to have him make love to her.

Instead of accommodating her as any gentleman would, she remembered, smiling, he took his time. He'd begun kissing her on her toes and had worked his way up her legs. Once he reached her upper thighs she tried to close them but it was too late.

The magic of his fingers and tongue brought her to a surprisingly sudden and intense climax. Before her last involuntary tremor had ended, he was inside her, moving rapidly, until once again she tumbled over the edge of satisfaction, this time taking him with her.

She sighed at the memory. Each time they made love was better than the last, which she found amazing.

As soon as she dressed, Jenna went downstairs and found Ian already in the dining room, drinking coffee and reading the paper. He glanced up as she walked into the room and stood until she was seated. "Good morning," he said in his early-morning voice. "I hope you slept well," he added with a straight face.

She nodded, equally calm. "Yes, thank you. My mattress is extremely comfortable." She had fallen asleep sprawled across his chest, her head tucked into his shoulder.

Jenna poured her coffee and added some light fare to her plate. "Would you like something to eat?" she asked.

He folded the paper neatly and replied, "Yes. I'm starved, for some reason."

"I can't imagine why."

When they finished breakfast, Ian changed their routine somewhat by saying, "Before you get to work, I'd like to speak to you about something. In the library, please.

"Certainly. I'll meet you there."

Jenna went to her office to get a notepad. Men were such strange creatures, she mused. She had to struggle to keep her responses to him circumspect during the day, while he seemed to have no problem at all reverting back to his employer mode.

Perhaps all men kept their relationships compart-mentalized. The more deeply she fell in love with him, the more difficulty she had not greeting him in the morning with a kiss, or touching him whenever possible. With a mental shake, she picked up her pad and pen and went quietly into the library.

Ian knew exactly when she walked into the room, even though he stood across the room facing away from the door. He seemed to have a radar signal where she was concerned. When she was near, he could feel his body reacting to her presence. He was counting on the fact that she had a similar reaction to him.

He smiled. "You're prompt, as usual." Nodding to one of the chairs in front of the fireplace, he said, "Please sit. I believe we'll be more comfortable here."

He sat in the other chair and saw her steno pad. "You won't have to take notes," he said. "This is more of an off-the-record discussion."

She folded her hands and waited.

"I think we're making good progress on the new novel, don't you?"

"Yes, I do. You seem to have a clear idea of where the story is headed."

"I also received the copy of the contract this morning. Benson had it couriered to me." He massaged the back of his neck. "Chris Wood—you remember I mentioned he was a friend and lawyer— plans to be here tomorrow to look over the contract. It's for three books."

"Why, Ian, that's spectacular! Congratulations!"

"I called Todd to find out when I can return to

work. He told me to start next Monday, which means I'll be returning to London this weekend.''

''Everything is working out well for you. I'm glad.''

''Except for you.''

She looked at him, stunned by his comment. ''I don't understand. I thought you found my work satisfactory.''

He rubbed his forehead. This wasn't coming out the way he meant it. He leaned forward in his chair and touched her hands. They were icy.

''I don't want to go to London without you. Besides, we work well together. I want to continue with this newest book and I need your help. I know we've never talked about this but I really think we should get married. You'll come with me to London and meanwhile I'll work on getting a transfer to this area. I know you don't like cities, but at the moment I can't do anything about where I'll be working.''

Ian knew he was rambling but the expression on Jenna's face had frozen when he mentioned the word *marriage*. She stared at him as though she couldn't believe what he was saying.

He stumbled to a stop and sat looking at her. When she didn't respond he frowned and finally asked, ''Did I make myself clear?''

She continued to look at him with something less than a loving expression. ''Oh, yes,'' she finally said coolly. ''I believe you were quite clear. You need me to continue working for you, which will mean my moving to London with you. So you've asked me to marry you.''

Summed up in that fashion, his offer of marriage didn't sound the same way he meant it.

''Uh, yes, that's the gist of it, I suppose.''

''I never gave a thought to the possibility that you wanted a permanent relationship with me,'' she said quietly.

''Oh. Well, actually I never thought I'd ask anyone to marry me, either.'' He smiled ruefully. ''I've been a confirmed bachelor for many years. However, circumstances change. I realize that now.''

He tried to think of something romantic to say to her. He wished now that he had the ring so he could offer it to her. Not on bended knee, of course. She knew him well enough to know he wasn't one to get all mushy. He mapped out his goal and went after it.

Right now his goal was to get Jenna to marry him. Nothing complicated about that.

''So what do you think?''

''I think your arrogance is beyond belief.''

He straightened as though she had slapped him. ''My arrogance. What's so arrogant about asking you to marry me?''

''Your cavalier way of presenting the idea, for starters. As you say, you've been single for a long while. However, you've discovered that it would be more convenient to marry me, and I'm supposed to fall in with your plans.'' She stood and shook her head. "No, I will not marry you. Hire yourself another secretary in London!" She marched out of the room without another glance.

What had just happened? Ian shook his head in bewilderment. They'd been getting along so well. They were certainly compatible in bed. She had no family and as far as he knew, no other job.

What was wrong with her, anyway?

She acted as though he'd insulted her!

Well, that certainly put their relationship in a much clearer light. She was willing to go to bed with him, to have mind-blowing sex with him, but she did not want a permanent relationship with him.

If anyone should feel insulted, he should.

And he did. However, he had this tremendous ache in his chest at the thought that she intended to leave him.

He'd been so pleased when he'd come up with the idea. He would marry her. She would become a permanent part of his life…the most important. He was stunned by her reaction.

Unable to stay there another moment, Ian left the castle, got into his car and drove away, unable to face anyone.

As soon as she reached the hallway, Jenna sprinted to the top of the stairs, and then ran the rest of the way to her room as though the hounds of hell were nipping at her heels. Once inside, she shut the door and leaned against it. She shook, more from shock than because she was chilled.

The absolute last thing she'd expected this morning was to have Ian propose marriage. She had never considered their relationship, whether professional or personal, to be permanent. Of course she was in love with him and he probably knew that. In fact, he was no doubt counting on her to fall into his arms with relief and open adoration.

He'd made the offer as though negotiating a business contract. He might as well tattoo a serial number on her forehead and include her with the rest of his office furnishings when he moved.

Was that all she was to him? A convenience? She'd become a habit and he didn't want to bother creating new ones.

The more she thought about the scene she'd just left, the angrier she became. How dare he be so insensitive.

After taking several calming breaths, Jenna forced herself to return downstairs to her office. She closed and locked the door. She wasn't in the mood to see anyone, especially Ian.

She would transcribe his tapes because that was what she was paid to do. After that she would call Violet Spradlin. Her fantasy bubble had burst. She needed to put her relationship with Ian MacGowan behind her and get on with her life, marking him down as an experience not to be repeated.

Jenna began to work, ignoring the tears streaming down her face.

Chapter Thirteen

Jenna woke the next morning with a nasty headache and was greeted by dismal weather, which fitted her mood quite nicely.

She'd overslept, but it didn't matter. She had finished the tapes on her desk and meticulously cleaned her office before she came upstairs last night around two o'clock.

No one disturbed her while she worked. When she went into the kitchen for something to eat, only Cook was there. Jenna wasn't in the mood to see Hazel right away, either.

She felt as though all the tender feelings she had for Ian had been trampled. He had used her feelings for him to get her to agree to his business proposition.

It certainly hadn't been a proposal by any stretch of the imagination.

She'd been so careful never to let on how deeply she loved him. She was thankful for that, at least. The humiliation would be more than she could bear.

The rain let up after breakfast. Since she had nothing in her office to do and refused to seek out Ian, Jenna put on her rain slicker and went out to the gardens.

Eventually, the sun peeked through the clouds. She removed her rain gear and took the path that led to the front of the castle. As she rounded the corner she saw a flashy red sports car wheel into the courtyard and stop.

She stood and watched as a man—whom she guessed was Chris Wood—got out of the sports car and looked around. He was tall and lean. She saw him stretch and hold his back as he moved his spine. When he saw her he said, "You look like a garden fairy. Are you real?"

She laughed. "Very real, thank you. You must be Chris Wood. I'm Jenna Craddock." When she reached him, she held out her hand. He took it, his blue eyes studying her intently.

"I know this sounds lame, but haven't we met before?"

"No."

"You're certain?"

"Absolutely. I would remember you." She only spoke the truth because Chris was a very striking man. His blond hair fell across his forehead in a boyish way and his eyes promised all kinds of mischief. In short, she liked him on sight.

He frowned. "Strange, though. Give me a moment and I'll place you."

They turned and walked toward the front door. "Are you visiting Ian?" he asked.

"I've been working for him for several months. The job was temporary, transcribing, and I would guess we're through with that part."

"If you're looking for work, look no further… I'll hire you."

She laughed. "Of course you will. And what makes you think I would be qualified?"

"Simple. If you've put up with Ian and his surly moods, I'll put you in charge of calming irate and difficult clients. What do you say?" He opened the front door and stepped back for her to enter.

"Thank you for your kind offer, Mr. Wood, but—"

"Chris," he inserted smoothly.

"Chris," she obediently repeated, "but I think I'll take a few weeks off before I consider taking another job." They paused in the foyer and she was disconcerted by his intent stare.

He pulled a card from his wallet. "Well, if you ever change your mind, give me a ring." With a breezy salute he headed toward the library. Jenna was halfway up the stairs when she heard him shout, "I've got it!" He turned and strode toward her.

"What do you have?" she asked, amused despite herself.

"You look just like a picture!"

"Come again?"

"You were correct. I haven't seen you before, but I have seen a painting of you, hanging in a place of honor at the home of Sir Douglas Gordon. I was visiting him at his place last fall. You must be kin."

Jenna went down a few steps until she was eye level with him. "I've never heard of him."

"It's astounding, the resemblance, now that I've placed it," he said, looking at her in wonder. "I *knew* you looked familiar. There has to be some kind of connection between you and the Gordon portrait. The resemblance is too pronounced to be a coincidence."

Jenna's heart began to race. "Where does Sir Douglas live?"

Chris laughed. "You probably won't believe me, but he has a beautiful home on an island located near Oban. The family's lived there for centuries. You know the kind of place," he added, sweeping his arm to encompass their surroundings.

"How old is he?" she asked, determined to sound calm. Otherwise, he would be convinced she was bonkers.

"Sir Douglas?" he asked, glancing toward the ceiling before saying, "Oh, I would say a comfortable middle age, although he's certainly stayed fit."

His gaze fell on her. "You're serious, aren't you? You really don't know him?"

"'Fraid not."

"Then the painting must be of your twin sister, is all I can say." He glanced at his watch. "It's been a pleasure meeting you, Jenna Craddock, and I can rest easy now that I've managed to place you."

Jenna continued on her way upstairs, her mind awhirl with possibilities. Here was yet another person who saw a striking resemblance between her and a woman, between her and a portrait.

Perhaps Fiona was the woman in the painting. Stranger things had happened. She hurried to her room and began to pace.

Was it possible that she might be related to Sir Douglas Gordon? If not, maybe he could tell her who the woman in the painting was. Of course, the only way to find out was to contact him, explain who she was and ask if he would see her. She could do that. Of course she could. But did she dare?

She felt the excitement bubble inside her. She now had two leads—if she wanted to follow up on them—that might explain why Mr. Dumas had been looking for her.

Unable to stay in her room another moment, she hurried out to find Hazel. After all, she had to share this news with somebody!

"Good God, man, it's as dark as a cave in here!" Chris said when Ian called for him to enter. "Let's open the drapes, shall we? The weather's turned out quite nicely considering how it was earlier.''

Without waiting for a response, Chris strode to the windows and French doors, and opened the drapes. "There," he said, turning back to where Ian sat behind his massive desk.

"How's the leg and knee?" he asked, sprawling into one of the chairs in front of the desk. "You look a little pale. The leg still giving you problems?"

Ian scrubbed his eyes with the heels of his hands. "Only when it rains, Chris." He scratched his unshaven jaw. "It's good to see you."

"On closer inspection, you look like hell. When's the last time you've been to bed?"

A sudden memory of reluctantly leaving Jenna's bed early yesterday morning flashed in his head. "I was drowning my sorrows last night, okay? Could you speak a little softer, and for pity's sake, close some of those drapes?"

Chris hopped up and half closed the drapes. "Why were you drowning your sorrows? I thought you'd be over the moon with a contract to buy your novel in hand. I figured we'd be busy celebrating, not conducting some kind of wake."

Ian ran his hand through his hair. He didn't want to discuss Jenna with Chris. He didn't want to discuss Jenna with anyone. He wished there was some type of operation where a surgeon could permanently remove her from his brain.

"It's nothing I can't deal with," he finally replied. He picked up the contract from his side table and handed it to Chris. "This is what they're offering. What do you think?"

"This is the contract? I thought it was your manuscript. If I've got to sit and read this, you'd better offer me some sustenance."

Ian looked at his watch and noted the time. "I'll have Cook prepare one of your favorite meals. It's the least I can do."

"Don't worry. I intend to bill you for my time," Chris said with a chuckle. "Nothing comes free, you know."

"No," Ian agreed soberly, "I know."

"Hazel, do you have a minute?" Jenna said, meeting her on the stairs.

"I was coming to get you. You have a visitor in the sitting room."

"Me? Who would be here to see me?"

"I didn't ask. What did you need?"

"Oh! Nothing, really. Some news I received that I thought I'd share. It will keep." When she paused at the bottom of the stairs to check her appearance in the mirror there, she heard the murmur of male voices coming from the library. Jenna swallowed. None of Ian's business had anything to do with her anymore. She just wished the pain she felt whenever she thought of him would go away.

She straightened her spine, plastered a polite smile on her face and walked into the room.

The first thing Jenna saw when she opened the door to the sitting room was a young redheaded woman, sitting before the fireplace. Jenna could only see her profile. She looked relaxed and comfortable. Puzzled, Jenna walked over to her.

"I understand you wish to see me?"

The woman quickly glanced up. When she saw Jenna, she stood and Jenna realized that she was at least four months pregnant. Jenna glanced back at the woman's face and froze.

She felt as though she were looking into a mirror. The woman's hair was redder than Jenna's, and her eyes were green, but those were minor differences.

Jenna realized that this must be Fiona MacDonald. "Oh, my. You must be Emily's friend," she said. "I can see now how she could have confused me for you."

The woman stared at her with such warmth that Jenna blinked.

"Oh my word," the woman said softly, her fingers against her lips. Tears flooded her eyes. "I've finally found you...after all this time. I truly believe in miracles."

"You know me?" Jenna said, her voice unsteady.

The woman cleared her throat. "I'm Fiona, as you guessed. I've gotten married since I last saw Emily. I'm Fiona Dumas...and I'm your sister."

Jenna sank into a chair. Dumas. Her last name was Dumas! "How can that be?"

"It's a long story that I'll be glad to tell you." Fiona sat, placing her hand on her abdomen. Jenna wondered if she was in shock. This could not be happening. After all of these months, she had finally met a family member.

"Emily called me last night," Fiona said. Her pleased smile was contagious. "She said her meeting with you had slipped her mind until now, but she thought I might be interested to hear about you. I came here as soon as I could." After a pause to wipe her eyes, Fiona cleared her throat and in a shaky voice said, "Your parents were Hedra and Tristan Craddock, who moved to Australia several years ago and were later killed in a flash flood. Am I right?"

How would anyone in Scotland know about her childhood? "How do you know about me when I've never heard of you?" she finally asked.

"My husband, Greg, is a private investigator. When he eventually found out that a couple in Cornwall adopted you, he went there in hopes of finding you."

"Morwenna mentioned when I first arrived in the U.K. that a Mr. Dumas from Edinburgh had been to visit her asking questions about me. However, I've had no luck finding him."

"Oooh, that woman! I could easily throttle her without remorse. She wouldn't even tell Greg your first name. Said she didn't recall. We've had investigators working in Australia ever since.'' She gave a watery laugh. ''And here you are, practically underneath our noses.''

''Morwenna's attitude really doesn't surprise me,'' Jenna said. ''You see, I had no idea I'd been adopted until she told me.''

''Oh, my. Well, at least each of the adopting couples was consistent about keeping the adoptions a secret.''

''What do you mean?''

''I know you're going to find this overwhelming, just as I did when I first learned about it. I'll try to be as coherent as possible.'' She reached for Jenna's hand, gazing at her with so much warmth and, yes, love that Jenna couldn't contain her emotion. Fiona said, ''I still can't believe we've finally found you.'' She brushed her hand across her eyes. ''Drat! Since I've been pregnant I cry over the least little thing, and this is far from little.''

Jenna dabbed at the moisture in her own eyes and tried to laugh. ''I can't blame my tears on a pregnancy. I'm having trouble comprehending all of this. I mean, how did your husband know I existed?''

Before Fiona could reply, Hazel brought in a tea tray and set it in front of them. Jenna poured and handed a cup to Fiona.

Once Hazel left, Fiona settled back into her chair and carefully sipped her tea, then said, ''Twenty-five years ago last November 28, you were born during the same night that two other baby girls were born."

"You mean I'm one of triplets?" Jenna said in disbelief.

"Yes. We both are. And we have another sister. If Kelly had felt better this morning, she would have come with me. You see, Kelly is our third sister and the one who started this search. She found me last winter and we've been looking for you ever since."

"Oh, my," Jenna managed to say over the lump that had suddenly filled her throat. "I have not one, but two sisters." She barely got the last word out before tears started flowing down her cheeks. They looked at each and began to laugh and cry at the same time. It took them a while before they were able to calm down enough to talk and to dry their eyes.

"Do you have any idea why I was the one placed for adoption," Jenna finally asked. She steeled herself for the answer.

"Oh, it wasn't just you. All three of us were adopted and none of us was told that we were adopted or one of triplets. If Kelly, who used to live in New York, by the way, hadn't accidentally come across her adoption papers and sent an investigator to Edinburgh to talk with the solicitor who handled the adoptions, we would never have found each other."

"Why wouldn't someone want triplets? I'd be delighted to have babies, no matter what."

"So was Moira. Our mother. She loved us dearly but she'd just suffered through the tragedy of seeing her husband killed in a fight with his brother. She ran away and stopped in Craigmor. You see, my father was a doctor and he delivered us, even though he was semiretired at the time.

"Moira lived barely a week after we were born. She begged my father to find good homes for us but not to keep us together in case our uncle came looking for triplets, which he probably did. So in a way, my dad and the solicitor, Mr. McCloskey, saved our lives. The MacDonalds adopted me, a couple named MacLeod from New York took Kelly and the Craddocks took you. None of us was ever supposed to find out."

"But that's horrible to keep us away from each other."

"I know. Kelly and I were very angry with the MacLeods and MacDonalds for being so secretive. They could have told us once we were grown. As it turned out, by the time we found out, our parents had died."

"Just as mine had."

"Yes, but you lost yours much, much too young. We've wondered what happened to you, if you were adopted again and if your name had been changed. When Emily mentioned meeting a woman by the name of Craddock who looked just like me, I knew it had to be you!"

"This is truly unbelievable."

"I know. I wanted to find you the minute I spoke to her last night—thank goodness you told her where you lived—but I needed to make some arrangements first. Greg won't be home until possibly tomorrow and our daughter Tina is with Kelly, who is ready to have her baby in a few weeks."

"You have a daughter?" Jenna asked wistfully.

Fiona smiled. "She's six years old and I don't know how I ever managed without her. She's Greg's daughter. Her mother died when she was barely two. Greg and I met because Kelly hired him to find her parents. The investigation led him to me."

Jenna glanced at Fiona's gently rounded lap. "And when was that?" she asked with a smile.

"About eight months ago, actually. We had a double wedding in March and we wanted so much to have you there."

Jenna fell back against her chair. "I was actually here in March. This is too much to take in."

"I know, and it hasn't helped that I've been so excited to see you that I've barely been coherent." She hesitated then said, "I don't know if you have time, but if you do, would you let me take you to Craigmor for a couple of days? You must meet Kelly and later Greg. I'm not certain when Nick—he's Kelly's husband—is supposed to return. Believe me, they're all going to be so excited to meet you at last. In fact, I'm almost afraid to return without you!"

Would it matter to Ian if she took off a few days?

She had no intention of disturbing his meeting to ask.

"I'd love to come," she said. She would deal with Ian, her boss, later. Ian, her lover, no longer had any sway over her. "Wait here and I'll pack an overnight bag."

"You might want to pack a little more, just in case. I promise I'll have you back here no later than a week."

"All right. I'll find Hazel and tell her my plans."

Jenna met Hazel coming out of the kitchen. "Hazel! You're never going to believe it, but Fiona is my sister!"

Hazel chuckled at Jenna's excitement. "Now I would never have guessed...since you look like two peas in a pod."

"Actually there's another one, as well," Fiona said, laughing. "I'm a triplet."

"You don't say! News like that certainly comes as a shock, now, doesn't it?"

"Fiona has suggested I come home with her to meet the rest of my family." Jenna hugged those words close to her heart. At last she had a real family. "I don't want to disturb Ian's meeting with Chris. Could you tell him that my sister came to visit and that I'll be with her for a few days? She lives in Craigmor. If he needs me before I get back, have him call me. I'll have Fiona give you her number."

"Don't be playing innocent with me. You want

me to tell him so you don't have to deal with his reaction.''

Jenna grinned. ''Well, that, too. Although I think he'll be relieved to have me out from underfoot for a few days.''

''Do you now? I wonder where you'd get an idea such as that? The man dotes on you, you know.''

''Not really. He just doesn't want to have to train yet another secretary once he leaves for London. He asked me to go with him.''

''He did, did he?''

''Yesterday. Since I've told him that I don't wish to live in a city, I can't believe he was surprised I said no.'' She gave Hazel a quick hug. ''I need to pack. Oh, this is so exciting,'' Jenna said, whirling away and dancing upstairs.

She rushed through packing and hurried downstairs, eager to see Fiona again. ''I'm ready,'' she announced, pausing in the doorway.

''Don't you need to tell your employer you're leaving?''

Jenna had the grace to blush. ''I left him a message with the housekeeper. We'll leave your number in case he needs to contact me for some reason.''

''Oh. Then shall we go? I can't tell you how excited I am to have found you. I know you're going to become tired of hearing me say that.''

''How could I?'' Jenna replied, laughing. ''I feel the same way. Finding sisters is beyond my most creative imaginings—and believe me when I tell you I'm highly imaginative!''

Once they were on the road to Craigmor, Fiona said, ''I know it's absolutely none of my business, but is there something going on between you and your boss?''

''No, there's nothing between us,'' Jenna replied, hoping that lightning wouldn't strike her for uttering such a bald-faced lie. ''Not really,'' she felt forced to add.

''Do you wish there were?''

Jenna tried to laugh but it came out as more of a sob. ''I know it sounds so trite to fall in love with your boss, but that's what I've done. But don't worry,'' she said hurriedly, ''I'll recover quickly enough.'' She glanced at Fiona's profile. ''Did I tell you he's moving back to London where he works? He's been recovering from an auto accident and has just been cleared to return to his regular duties. Plus he's written a book, a really wonderful book, actually. I helped transcribe it for him. He already has an offer from a publisher to buy it.''

Once Jenna stopped chattering, Fiona asked, ''How does he feel about you?'' Jenna bit down hard on her bottom lip to stop tears from forming. ''He likes me well enough, I suppose,'' she said, remembering the passionate way he made love to her. ''He'll find another secretary easily enough, I'm quite certain.'' *As well as someone to warm his bed,* she thought miserably.

"Whatever you say," Fiona said. "But something tells me I'm not hearing all of the story." She grinned. "Don't worry, I'll figure a way to pry it out of you. If not me, then Kelly will. Suddenly having two sisters to harass you will be something of a shock, I'm sure."

"Perhaps. But I'm looking forward to it."

Chapter Fourteen

"Are you telling me that you're considering not signing this contract?" Chris asked while sipping brandy after dinner that evening. They had returned to the library and were seated in front of the fireplace. "I find your hesitancy unfathomable. You can't convince me that you prefer to let the manuscript gather dust on a shelf somewhere after all these months of work you've put in."

Ian listened to his friend with half an ear. He was suffering from pangs of guilt for not inviting Jenna to join them for dinner. After putting up with Chris's periodic badgering for more information about his very attractive assistant, Ian had chosen not to share a meal where he'd have to watch and listen to Chris flirt with Jenna.

He'd been an ass yesterday, avoiding her all day as though not seeing her would make him feel any better. He wondered what he could do or say to convince her that even though she wasn't interested in marrying him, he wanted her to continue to work for him.

What had gotten into him, anyway, thinking she'd want to marry him? Perhaps because he'd never been tempted to ask a woman to marry him before, he must have thought, rather egotistically, that the proposal was a mere formality and that she would fall immediately into his arms, vowing her eternal love for him.

While sitting in his room last night drinking himself into a stupor, Ian had gone over each and every word spoken between them. Sometime during the night he'd realized that he hadn't actually verbalized his feelings for her.

Surely she already knew how he felt about her. Couldn't she conclude that he wouldn't ask her to marry him without loving her…rather desperately, as it turns out.

"Ian?"

"Hmm?"

"Have you heard anything I've said?"

"Yes, of course I have. You want to know if I intend to accept or reject this contract."

"Well, yes, that's true…I did say that about a half hour ago. What's the matter with you, anyway? You look like hell and seem not to care one way or another if you have a future as an author or not.''

"You think I should sign it, then?'' Ian replied.

"I think you should get down on your knees and thank God for such an opportunity. These people obviously see a strong future in publishing for you. They're committing to a marketing campaign that most authors would die for, not to mention paying you quite well for your first efforts. So what is the problem?''

"I don't like the idea of committing to produce three novels. I was willing to sign a contract for one and I've started a second one, but the thought of writing three is a little overwhelming.''

"We should all be so lucky.''

They sat in silence and Ian thought about what a good friend Chris had always been. Only now did Ian realize how much he relied on Chris, taking their friendship for granted. He sighed and said, "I've come to a crossroad in my life, Chris, and I'm at a loss what to do. For the first time that I can remember I don't have everything mapped out in front of me.''

"That's welcome news, I must say,'' Chris replied, smiling. "I don't remember a time since I've known you that you didn't know exactly what you wanted and how you intended to get it.''

"The thing is, I've been cleared to return to duty.'' Chris was one of a handful of people who knew what Ian did for a living. He would understand what that meant. "They're expecting me to report in on Monday. After that, I won't have much time to devote to writing."

"I'm sure that's true, but getting back to work as soon as possible has been your goal since you were injured. Hasn't it?"

"Yes. At first the writing was just something to do while I healed. I had no idea I would get so caught up in the process." He gave his head a quick shake. "What's worse, when I was through with it, I felt at loose ends until I started another book. I'm cleared to go back to work and yet..." He paused, thinking, then said, "Oh, I don't know. Ignore my meandering."

"Tell me something, Ian," Chris said, setting his brandy snifter on a nearby table, "are you actually contemplating resigning from the agency?"

"That would be crazy...." Another pause. "Wouldn't it?"

"Yes, if you're determined to continue risking your life and limbs. You've always said your career was with the agency. With your dedication, I've always believed you."

"So have I," Ian muttered. "So how can I, in good faith, sign a contract for three novels when I've only written one?"

"I can see your dilemma."

Would it make a difference to Jenna if he were to resign, or would she care? What did he know about females, anyway? He supposed that most women went for the romantic scene…flowers, jewels, fine wine, candlelight. But that wasn't who he was. He didn't have a romantic bone in his body. Jenna knew that.

Her passionate response to his lovemaking had made him think that she loved him. How naive was that? He'd never considered marriage with the other women he'd been involved with, never expected them to be in love with him. What if all she'd wanted from him was experience in bed?

"So what do you intend to do?" Chris said, breaking into Ian's reverie.

Absently, Ian replied, "I suppose I need to speak to her about all of this and—"

"Speak to whom?"

Shocked by what he'd said aloud, Ian said, "I meant I need to speak to Todd before making any decisions." He took a sip of his cognac. "Did I mention that his first suggestion was to put me behind a desk?"

Chris laughed. "Now that's funny. You're too active for that, which is one of the reasons I'm surprised you enjoy writing so much."

Ian smiled. "I'm seldom behind a desk. I pace, I talk into my portable recorder. I go for hikes. I'm all over the place, which means I need a proficient assistant to transcribe my musings."

"Ah. Then you expect to have Jenna, I believe her name is, with you for a long while, assuming, of course, you tell Todd you're ready to retire."

Jenna. Yes, he would very much like to have her around for a long while. He already missed her light-hearted teasing, the way the light brought out the red in her hair, the way she had of looking at him, her eyes dancing as though she was enjoying some private joke, probably on him. The way she moved beneath him, holding him and responding to him until he felt he would— Well, never mind what he felt.

It was time to sit down with her and apologize for his boorish behavior since his fiasco of a proposal.

"She seems to be under the impression that her job here is through," Chris said thoughtfully. "I wonder why?"

"What are you talking about?"

"When we met outside this morning, she explained that she would be taking a few weeks off before looking for work. As a matter of fact, I offered her a job."

"The hell you did!" Ian lunged to his feet. "She has a job with me for as long as she wants, do you hear me? I'll go tell her that right now."

"Well," Chris said, rising from his chair and stretching. "I've done all I can for you here. Short of some minor adjustments, I believe the contract is very fair. If you wish, I'll call Benson and discuss the possibility of a single-book contract."

"Hold off on that. I'll let you know my decision in a day or so."

"Good. Now go get some sleep. You look positively haggard."

Ian walked Chris to his car and watched until the taillights blinked out of sight. He turned and headed for the stairs.

He knocked on Jenna's door and waited for her to answer. When she didn't he opened the door and peeked inside. There was no sign of her. Closing the door, he went in search of Hazel.

"Where's Jenna?" he demanded as soon as he saw her.

"Oh, yes. She told me to tell you but you've been rather busy today. She didn't want to disturb you so I decided to wait, myself."

"Tell me what?" he asked through gritted teeth.

"Well, it's like some kind of fairy tale. She isn't exactly Cinderella, but as you know she's been alone most of her life. Then out of the blue she discovers that she has two sisters...and they're triplets! Doesn't that beat all? It seems they were separated at birth but all a person needs to do is to see them together to recognize the strong resemblance."

"Are you saying she's gone?" he asked hoarsely, panic gripping him.

"She said she'd be back in a few days. She's gone to Craigmor, where her sisters live. You see, one of them came looking for her this morning and—" Hazel stopped speaking because Ian had left.

He stood in front of the fireplace in his room,

staring morosely into it. So she had family in Scotland, after all. He was happy for her. He really was, but he felt such a devastating loss at the knowledge that she'd already been planning to leave when Chris had arrived this morning. Now that she had found her family, she had a stronger reason to leave him behind.

At least she'd have to return for her belongings. They were still in her room, which was some consolation.

All right. He would wait until she returned and they would talk. He would get her to tell him how she felt and what she wanted to do. If he thought it would do any good, he'd tell her how much he loved her and needed her, and how, when she wasn't around, a large chunk of his heart was gone, as well.

In the meantime, all he could do was wait.

Chapter Fifteen

Jenna wanted to pinch herself to make certain she wasn't dreaming. Here she was, riding in a car driven by her sister. A sister! To think that her hope had been to find a distant cousin of sorts when she'd heard about Fiona. To have found a sister was an absolute miracle.

They had been silent for several minutes when Fiona gave Jenna a quick glance and sighed with obvious pleasure. "I can't tell you how excited I am that you could return to Craigmor with me today. I may not let you out of my sight for a month!"

"At least you were aware that I existed. I'm still in shock to discover I actually have a family. Belonging to a family has been my dream since I was a child."

"Tell me about growing up in Australia. I want to learn everything about you." Since Jenna had been thinking the same thing about Fiona, she could understand her interest.

"I'm afraid I don't remember much of my early childhood—just a few scenes that are indelibly etched in my mind. I understand I was five when we moved from Cornwall. I don't remember much about that time. I was told the small town where we lived was about an hour's drive from Sydney. My dad was a cabinetmaker. I'm not certain whether I actually remember seeing him in his shop or whether I imagine it. My memories of Mom are equally vague, although I do remember her in our kitchen. She wore an apron and made mouthwatering things that I loved to eat."

"Is it too painful to talk about how they died?"

"Again, I'm not certain whether I actually remember or I was told what happened. Piecing together everything, I know that the three of us were on holiday and were camping in the outback. I don't remember much about the area or what it looked like.

"After I was grown I looked through the file the orphanage kept on me. I wanted to find out what had actually happened. I found a newspaper article in my file. According to the investigators, my parents had chosen to set up camp in a swale, among some trees that fed on the moisture of what my parents thought was a dry riverbed. They hadn't lived in Australia long enough to understand the damage sudden torrents of rain can cause, you see. The only reason I survived was because I slept in the van. At least that's what the authorities decided.

"Sometime during the night a sudden rainstorm hit. When the water started down the surrounding slopes to the low place where we were camped, the torrent swept away everything but the van. Everything...including the tent and my parents.

"My one strong recollection was waking up to find a black face with strange white markings staring at me through the window. I screamed and called for my mom and dad. I was paralyzed with fear. Then the head disappeared." She looked over at Fiona. "I had nightmares about that for years... seeing a scary face and being afraid...calling for my parents and they never come to save me."

"Was the face some kind of mask?"

"Oh, no. He was an Aborigine. A group of them were hunting the morning after the storm and they came across the debris from our camp. They recovered my parents' bodies and some of them carried the bodies to the nearest town. The rest of them went searching for possible survivors. I owe them my life. I wouldn't have survived for long out there."

"What happened after you screamed?"

"When they saw how hysterical I was, they contacted the authorities who came for me, I was told. I don't remember that part. Just the face, staring at me through the window."

"How horrible. Where did you go after that?"

"The authorities sent me to Sydney and placed me in the orphanage. I don't know how long I was there until I was placed in a foster home. I was moved a couple of times for various reasons that I don't recall. One of my first memories was sitting in a corner reading. I suppose I used books as an escape. Caseworkers said they never had a complaint about me, but that's probably because I retreated into my own world that I'd peopled with characters I'd learned about from books. I've often been told I have too vivid an imagination. That's probably true, although my imagination kept me from feeling quite so alone."

When Fiona didn't comment, Jenna glanced at her and saw tears rolling down her cheeks. "I'm sorry. I shouldn't have upset you."

"Don't mind me. I've been a watering pot since I became pregnant. It's a hormonal thing and quite normal, just embarrassing at times. It's just that I feel so sad that you were so far away and so alone all of this time. Perhaps the adults that made such life-altering decisions for the three of us thought they were doing the best thing by separating us, but it breaks my heart that Kelly and I weren't there to comfort and console you."

"I used to dream about having a family with brothers and sisters, aunts and uncles. That was my reason for returning to the U.K. Of course I didn't know I was adopted at the time."

"I'm glad you came. Even if you had to face that horrid woman in Cornwall."

"You mean, Morwenna the witch? She really didn't bother me…just her news. Actually, she reminded me of one of the matrons at the orphanage."

She grinned at Fiona and they began to laugh.

When they stopped for petrol and something to eat, they were amused to find that they ordered the same meal. It didn't take long for them to discover that they shared many likes and dislikes.

At one point, Fiona said, "You know, Kelly and I have already gone through this and it's eerie how much alike the three of us are. I can hardly wait to get back to Craigmor. Kelly's waiting at my home. She often stays with me while Nick's traveling. She used to go with him. Then her doctor grounded her until after the baby's born. She's very impatient, you know."

"Really?" Jenna said, sounding amused. "I wonder where she acquired that trait?"

Fiona's eyes danced. "Not from me, I can assure you. You can see how patient I am. As soon as Emily Gillis finally remembered to call me, I could scarcely sleep for wanting to come find you."

Jenna reached for Fiona's hand. "I'm so glad you did. Even though I had your name and the town where you used to live, I suppose I was afraid of another Morwenna-type shooing me away from her door at the mere question of possible kinship."

"That will never happen."

They finished their meal and continued on their journey. Jenna's stomach tightened when Fiona said, "How did it happen that you're living in Scotland? How did you find the position with Ian?"

Jenna didn't want to be reminded of Ian. She swallowed and in a neutral voice explained about Ms. Spradlin and how Jenna came to be hired. "He's gruff and can be downright grumpy at times. I'm not certain if that's his regular personality or the one he adopted while he was convalescing from his injuries."

"Oh, my. How did you put up with him?"

"For one thing, I'm not easily intimidated. The wife of my boss in Sydney used to say she didn't know how I managed to put up with her husband's moods. Neither Ian nor Mr. Fitzgerald are what a person would call charming and outgoing. The two men shared a great many traits. When I wrote Mr. Fitzgerald's wife to tell her so, she was really quite amused."

"I'm amazed you fell in love with Ian, from that description. I don't know how he could resist falling in love with you. We'll have to figure a way to have him on his knees begging you to stay…maybe offering marriage."

"He already has."

"Don't say things like that when I'm driving!" Fiona said. "What are you saying? He wants to marry you, you're in love with him and you said no? I can see me introducing you to Kelly. Kelly, meet our sister, the idiot.''

''I know how strange my decision must sound to you. The thing is, I've spent my life wanting to be loved, truly loved, by someone. Not tolerated, not patronized, not considered a convenience. Loved. I made a promise to myself when I was at last on my own that I would not, regardless of the provocation, marry anyone who did not love me.''

''And you're positive Ian doesn't love you.''

''Let's just say that Ian may be in lust with me. But love? No, I don't think so.''

''Perhaps he needs you to teach him how to love.''

Jenna looked at Fiona in surprise. ''I never looked at it that way.''

''I've discovered that by and large, men tend to bury their emotions. If he proposed, you know he must care deeply for you.''

''He made it sound like a business decision.''

''He may have sounded that way but maybe that's not how it felt to him.''

''You know, you're right. When I get back, I'll talk to him about the conversation. Instead of immediately being insulted, I'll seek out his reasons for asking me—besides needing a secretary for the foreseeable future.''

''Good. Communication is important. You should have been around this time last year when Greg and I were dealing with our situation. It wasn't bad enough that he lived in New York and I live here, that he was widowed with a small daughter. No, I didn't make it clear to him that I wanted him and was willing to fight to overcome the obstacles that might stand in the way of our being together.''

''So how did you end up together?''

Fiona grinned. ''Greg discovered it was more painful to let me go than it was to allow himself to love again.''

''I wonder if Ian could feel that way.''

''Look at it this way…you're giving him the opportunity to find out this week, aren't you?''

Fiona was right, Jenna thought as they pulled into the pretty village of Craigmor. She was eager to meet her family. However, she wanted to see Ian again. This time she wouldn't be shy about asking him how he felt about her. When she knew there was no chance for them, she would be able to put the past behind her and move on.

Why did she have to fall in love with such a complicated man?

Chapter Sixteen

The reunion that afternoon between the three women filled Fiona's home with laughter and tears, a few shrieks of surprise and a great deal of hugging as each of them shared her life story to the present.

Jenna met the delightful Tina Dumas. If Jenna hadn't known better, she would have thought that Fiona had given birth to Tina. Their love for each other was readily apparent.

She heard the details about the courtship between Fiona and Greg. She laughed until she cried at Kelly's droll recital of her off-again on-again relationship with Dominic Chakaris, who, as her sisters assured Jenna, had much too much money to be good for him.

Fiona explained she had forgiven him his arrogance when she discovered how much he truly loved Kelly. Eventually she prompted Jenna to tell Kelly about Ian and Jenna was soon regaled with advice from both women, sometimes while they were talking at the same time.

Once Tina was in bed that evening, they settled into a more sober mood.

Fiona said, "You know, Jenna, I've been thinking about this since you told me about your parents. My parents were also drowned, although I was an adult when it happened. The pain is just the same, though. Does it make you wonder if there was some cosmic tie that caused each couple to drown together?"

Kelly spoke up in her no-nonsense tone. "Of course not. My parents were at home when they had their heart attacks."

Jenna's eyes widened. "Together?" she asked in astonishment.

When Kelly and Fiona stopped laughing at her reaction, Kelly said more soberly. "No. About four years apart. I think Mother grieved herself to death after Dad died. Maybe it was a good thing that your parents were together at the end."

Kelly yawned. "I'm sorry to break up our sister session but I'm going to have to go to bed. The larger this baby gets, the more insistent he becomes about having more room. Right now he's making it clear he's ready for me to get horizontal."

Fiona stood and offered Kelly her hand. When

Kelly made it to her feet, she said, "Fiona, I promise to do the same for you when you get to be this size," and all three of them laughed.

"When are you due?" Jenna asked.

"About six weeks or so. Isn't that ridiculous, considering my size? He'll probably be born walking and kicking the soccer ball I swear he has in there."

"So it's a boy?"

"I think so, but I don't know for sure. Nick and I don't care about the gender and we rather like the idea of not finding out until he—or she—arrives."

"Speaking of Nick," Fiona said, "have you talked to him today?"

"Of course. He called not long after you left. I didn't have a chance to tell him that we'd found Jenna before he hurriedly told me he loved me, made certain I was all right and said he would get home as soon as possible."

"You both miss your husbands very much. It shows in everything you say. I'm glad you're both so happy."

"We do, and we are. Thank goodness Greg doesn't travel as much as Nick does. He always tells me not to worry when he doesn't make it home when he hoped to get here. This is me, not worrying," Fiona added, crossing her eyes and letting her tongue hang out the side of her mouth. "He did say he'd be here soon. He can't get here too soon for me."

While Kelly prepared for bed and stretched out

beneath the covers, Fiona and Jenna sat at the end of her bed while Jenna answered Kelly's questions about Ian.

As she talked about him, she recalled how much he'd changed since she first met him, how he had responded to her and how she'd discovered the wry sense of humor hidden beneath his gruffness.

She described to them the party in London without discussing their ending up in bed together. She told them about the castle and the gardens, about Cook and Hazel and how much she had enjoyed her time there.

When she grew quiet, Kelly looked at Fiona. "She really has it bad, doesn't she?"

Fiona nodded. "We have to take her back in a day or two. That will be our chance to size him up and see if he's good enough for her. If we decide he is, he won't stand a chance. We'll see to that."

Jenna slipped off the bed and said, "You may find he isn't as malleable as you think."

"I'm counting on the fact that he's crazy in love with you and will listen to any advice we give him on how to win you over."

Kelly fluttered her fingers. "We'll enchant him for you and he'll never know what hit him."

Fiona added, "Yes, we'll convince him we're two pregnant sprites there to sprinkle our fairy dust over him to make him irresistible."

Jenna grinned. "Too late. It's already happened."

She went to bed that night and hugged a pillow

to her chest, wishing it were Ian. After spending the past few weeks sleeping with him, she was having trouble getting to sleep. Again. After the sleepless night she'd just spent she hoped sheer exhaustion would help her to rest.

She missed him so much. What if he really did love her? What if it was she who had misunderstood his motive for proposing to her? If so, her refusal must have hurt him.

Oh, dear.

Her last waking thought was to decide to return to the castle tomorrow. She couldn't tolerate the thought that she might have caused him pain. If she had misinterpreted his motive, she owed him a tremendous apology.

Jenna woke up the next morning with a start, confused at first by the commotion she heard downstairs. She could hear the surprised voices and laughter of her sisters, Tina's childish giggle as well as the rumble of men's voices.

The husbands were home.

Jenna hurriedly dressed and went downstairs.

The voices came from the kitchen. When she peeked in, she saw Fiona making breakfast, Kelly setting the table and little Tina sitting in the lap of one of the men, relating to him information that needed extravagant gestures for the proper telling. He appeared suitably enthralled.

Both men were slightly turned away from her so

that she couldn't see their faces. When Fiona reached for something in the cabinet, she saw Jenna and winked.

"Oh, Greg, honey, in all the excitement of you two showing up so early this morning, I forgot to mention that I solved one of your cases for you."

All conversation ceased. Fiona and Kelly wore identical smiles.

"How's that?"

"I got a lead, checked it out and made the connection."

Nick glanced at Greg, so that Jenna saw his classic Greek profile. All she could think was *Wow*. "Maybe you should hire her as one of your assistants," Nick said. "That is, if you can manage not to keep her pregnant all the time."

"You're one to talk," Greg retorted, and all of them laughed.

"Here's the result I got," she said, beckoning Jenna inside. The men looked toward the door. As soon as they saw her they stood, Greg still holding Tina in his arms.

"I can't believe it," Greg muttered in disbelief, setting Tina on her feet. "You must be—"

The three sisters spoke together. "Jenna Craddock."

"Where—and how—did you find her?" Nick asked, continuing to stare at her in amazement.

Everyone began to speak at once while Fiona poured Jenna coffee and Kelly pulled out the sixth chair at the table and nodded to Jenna. Everyone gathered around the table for breakfast.

"If we'd only known it, Jenna was close enough to have come to our weddings," Kelly said, and the explanations began.

After the sisters had brought the men up to date, Nick said, "There's no mistaking your kinship. Except for a little variation in your hair and eye colors, I wouldn't be able to tell any of you apart."

Kelly laughed. "I believe our bellies might give us away, Nick. Don't you?"

He pulled her to him by hooking his elbow around her neck. "You know what I mean," he said roughly, then shook his head and laughed. "You can be such a pain at times."

She batted her lashes at him. "And you love it."

He tilted his head for a second before nodding. "Well, yes. I'll give you that," he said, a wicked gleam in his eyes.

After breakfast and when Greg returned from taking Tina to visit her grandmother, the family gathered in the living room so that the men could become acquainted with Jenna.

Their presence made her miss Ian so much. As thrilled as she was to have discovered her sisters, she ached to talk to Ian and discuss whether they had a future together.

Nick explained once again, this time to Jenna, how he'd ended his meeting after talking to Kelly. "I decided I didn't care if this merger took place or not. I missed Kelly and felt I needed to be here for her. I left a trusted officer in charge.''

"As for me," Greg said, taking up the story, "I missed my flight yesterday. Otherwise I would have been home last night. I decided to call Nick and find out when he planned to return home. He was already on his way to the airport and offered me a ride…which I accepted, of course.''

The women sat next to their husbands on two love seat sofas facing each other. Jenna occupied one of the overstuffed chairs facing the fireplace.

Eventually, Greg said, "It's a shame, really, that Moira and Douglas never had the chance to watch their daughters grow to be such well-rounded, intelligent and beautiful women.''

"Douglas?" Jenna repeated, a bell suddenly clanging in her head. "Our father's name was Douglas?" Her voice had gone up a notch. "I can't believe I forgot! So much happened yesterday that I didn't remember what I heard until now.''

"What did you hear?" Fiona asked, puzzled by Jenna's sudden excitement.

"Douglas. Or to be accurate, Sir Douglas Gordon. If our father's name was Douglas, there's a good chance he may still be alive!''

The others looked at her as though she'd suddenly begun to babble nonsense.

"I know I sound demented and I apologize for not remembering sooner. I'd never heard our father's name until just now. All I was told was that my mother's name was Moira. I suppose I thought no one knew our father's name.''

''What have you found out?'' Kelly asked, her eyes round.

''Ian's friend and attorney, Chris Wood, came to see him yesterday. When he saw me he asked me if I was any kin to Douglas Gordon. He'd been to Sir Douglas's home and had seen a large portrait of a woman who he said could have been me!''

They looked at each other. Finally, Fiona said to Greg, ''Do you think he could possibly be—?'' She left the question unfinished.

''There's always that chance, honey, but let's not get our hopes up just yet.'' He turned to Jenna. ''Did you find out anything about him? Where he lives? How old he is? If he has any family?''

''Chris said that Sir Douglas lives on an island near Oban,'' she said slowly. ''He's middle-aged, but we didn't discuss family. We didn't talk long. An hour or so later Fiona arrived and I forgot everything else in the excitement of meeting her.''

Greg said, ''That gives me enough to work on. I'll see what I can find out. We want to be sure we're talking about the same person before announcing to the man that he has three daughters he's never seen.''

''It can't be the same person,'' Kelly pointed out in a reasonable tone. ''Remember? The reason Moira ran away was *because she saw his brother kill Douglas!*''

"Yes," Greg agreed. "That's what she thought she saw. But what if Douglas didn't die. If she ran as soon as it happened, all she knew for sure was that he'd been attacked and severely injured. But what if, in fact, he managed to recover?"

Nick said doubtfully, "It's a nice thought but I don't think it's likely. If his brother was intent on killing him, the brother would have made certain he'd accomplished the deed."

"Still," Kelly said wistfully, "it would be worth following up on, don't you think? This Sir Douglas doesn't have to know anything about us if he isn't the one who married Moira. I think Greg's right. We need to check this out."

The next hour was filled with speculation and various theories for what could have happened. Fiona's adopted parents were the only ones who had met Moira and heard her story and they were gone. Only the solicitor was alive to relate the tale secondhand.

A knock at the front door stopped their discussion, "I'll get it," Greg said.

Jenna heard the front door open.

"Yes?" Greg said.

"I'm looking for Jenna Craddock. Is she here?"

Ian! He was here! Jenna leaped up and ran out into the hallway.

Ian saw her past Greg's shoulder and smiled with what appeared to be relief. "Ian! What are you doing here? I was planning to return today." She turned to Greg. "Sir Ian MacGowan is my employer.'' Did Ian flinch just now? She wondered. If so, why?

Greg stepped back. ''Come in, Sir Ian. We're having a family celebration. You're welcome to join us.''

Jenna could see Ian's reluctance and knew how he dreaded such things. Impulsively, she took his hand and led him into the living room. ''Everyone,'' she said, grinning, ''this is Ian MacGowan, the man who offered me a home and a position when I first came to Scotland. Ian, this is Greg Dumas, who's married to my sister Fiona, and Nick Chakaris, who's married to my sister Kelly.''

Ian shook both men's hands and stared at the women. ''Unbelievable,'' he finally said. ''One of Jenna is about all one man can handle. But three?''

When the men laughed, the sisters looked at each other, puzzled by the remark and laughter.

''I'll admit it takes some getting used to,'' Nick admitted, earning a punch on his shoulder from his loving wife. He winced but Jenna saw the amusement in his eyes—and the love.

''Come and join us,'' Greg said, motioning to one of the chairs. ''Nick and I arrived this morning and the women have been bringing us up to date on their reunion.''

''May I get you some tea?'' Fiona asked.

Ian shoved his hands into his pockets, a muscle in his jaw flexing. ''I'd like to visit with you a little later. Right now, it's important that I speak with

Jenna.'' Jenna thought he looked like a trapped fox surrounded by a pack of hounds.

"If you'll excuse us," she said to her family, and smiled at Ian. She led the way to the back of the hallway and into a small sitting room cluttered with sewing material.

"Please excuse the clutter," she said nervously. "Fiona and Kelly are busy making baby clothes in here, as you can see. They decided to limit the mess by confining their efforts to one room."

Ian looked around the room, noting each partially completed project before turning his attention back to her. "I'm sorry if I've interrupted your visit. I would have waited for you to return but Hazel told me she wasn't certain when you'd be back."

Jenna motioned for him to sit, then sat nearby, facing him. "That's my fault, I'm afraid. I was so shocked and excited to meet Fiona that when she asked me to come back here with her, I couldn't say no." He looked tired, she thought. His hair stood up in little tufts of curls and she had an almost irresistible urge to smooth them down for him. When he didn't comment, she said, "I'm truly sorry I rushed out of there without telling you why. I didn't want to disturb your meeting with Chris."

"Chris said you plan to find another job," he said starkly. "Is that true?"

"At the time I spoke with him, yes. However, I've had more time to think about things since then, and no, I don't intend to leave."

He leaned back in his chair with a sigh. "Thank God."

"Is that why you're here?"

He straightened and rubbed his hands over his face. "I'm not good with words," he said abruptly.

"That's surprising, really, considering you recently finished an entire novel."

"About my feelings," he added.

"Ah."

"I went about everything wrong the other day. I've been kicking myself around the castle ever since, wishing I'd said things differently."

"What things?"

He stared at her for the longest time without speaking and she was convinced he'd gone mute. When he did speak, his stark words shocked her.

"I love you, Jenna. I probably fell in love with you the first time we met. I love you so much that I'm unable to function when you aren't there. I dream about you…when I can fall asleep at all. I reach for you in the night for comfort…and ache when you aren't there. I didn't ask you to marry me so I'd have a permanent secretary. I asked because I cannot conceive of a life without you."

Tears filled her eyes. "I love you, too, Ian."

He stared at her in surprise. Wearing an endearing, lopsided smile, he said, "You do?"

"Oh, yes. I would never have made love with you if I wasn't totally and irrevocably in love with you."

"Yet you said you wouldn't marry me."

She smiled through her tears. "Yes. Silly of me, I know. I had some preconceived idea of how a proposal should be. Since you never mentioned your feelings, I decided you didn't love me. Only later did I recall all the things you've said and done, how eager you are to hold me, to make love to me, to humor me. I was being very immature and I'm sorry."

He reached into his shirt pocket and pulled out a ring. "If you want me to, I'll offer this to you on bended knee. Whatever it takes to convince you to marry me."

Jenna left her chair and fell into his lap, kissing him while punctuating each kiss with the words, "Yes, I'll marry you."

He held her tightly against him and she felt the tension leave him. He took her finger and slipped on the ring. "I guessed at your ring size."

Jenna kept her head on his shoulder while she admired his choice. "It fits beautifully," she said with a sigh. She pulled back slightly so that she could see his face. "You need to understand that by marrying me you're taking on a great many more family members than either of us could have known about."

"Does that mean I have to get their permission before you'll marry me?" he asked in dismay.

She laughed at him. "It probably wouldn't hurt," she said. "They might want to know your prospects, whether you can support me, that sort of thing."

He stared at her in bewilderment. Finally, he muttered, "You're teasing me, aren't you?"

"Yes, although my sisters are actually very protective of me, I've discovered, which is such a novel experience for me. I have to admit I'm very touched by their attitudes. They may watch you very closely at first because they don't want to see me hurt."

"I never want to see you hurt, either, believe me. As God is my witness, I promise to love you and protect you for as long as I live."

She cupped his jaw with her hands. "Today you've said some of the most romantic things I've ever heard." Just before she kissed him, she said, "You know, you might want to try your hand at writing romance novels, as well."

Chapter Seventeen

Kelly spotted the ring on Jenna's finger as soon as Jenna and Ian walked back into the room. She winked at Fiona and said to Ian, "I suppose this means you're going to take her back home with you, even though she's only been here a day."

Ian laughed and hugged Jenna to his side. "I'm afraid so. However, we don't have to leave just yet. She mentioned something about the possibility the three of you have a father who's alive. I'd like to hear more about it."

"Before contacting the man directly," Greg said, "I'm going to find out more about him. If he is who we think he is, I'll contact him and see about setting up a meeting."

Nick said, "Meanwhile…welcome to the family, Ian." He held out his hand and Ian took it with a look of relief.

Jenna and Ian spent the rest of their visit listening and sharing histories and anecdotes with their new family.

"Thank you for coming to get me," Jenna said when Ian pulled into the driveway of the castle later that evening.

"Believe me, the pleasure was all mine."

When he helped her from the car, he kissed her. When he opened the door to his home, he kissed her. When he paused at the bottom of the stairs, he kissed her.

"You found her, I see," Hazel said.

Ian raised his head and looked at Hazel. "Go away," he said, and kissed Jenna again.

Hazel laughed. "I know you believe you can live on love, but some food wouldn't hurt you, either."

Ian sighed and stepped back from Jenna. "See what I mean? She's a nag and treats me like a child." They followed Hazel into the dining room.

"Only when you act like one," Hazel retorted. "I'll be right back."

Ian sat and pulled Jenna onto his lap. "Let's get married tomorrow." He nuzzled her neck.

"Ian! We can't do that. Your parents will want to be here and I'd like my family to attend, as well."

"Here we go," he said with resignation. "I

should have known. Planning a wedding isn't for a faint-hearted male. Just so you know, I refuse to wait until next spring or summer to marry you. You might change your mind. Or…another man might snatch you away.''

''Oh, I'm certain that's one of your biggest fears,'' she said dryly, shaking her head in exasperation.

''Let the poor lass eat,'' Hazel said, bringing a tray filled with everything they needed. She quickly set the table, set out steaming plates and filled two glasses with wine.

''So when's the date?'' Hazel asked. When they looked at her in surprise she nodded toward the ring. ''When you give her the MacGowan family engagement ring, I'm certain there's going to be a preacher here before long.''

Jenna looked at the ring on her finger. ''This is an heirloom?'' she asked, staring. ''I had no idea.''

''No reason for you to know,'' Ian replied, glaring at Hazel. ''Do you have to tell everything you know? I didn't want her to be nervous about wearing it.''

''Don't worry,'' Jenna said. ''I'll never take it off my finger!''

As soon as they finished eating, Ian hurried her to his rooms. Once inside the sitting room, he never slowed, but continued to his bedroom. ''You're sleeping in here from now on. You can take all the time you want to plan whatever wedding you want, but you're staying in here starting tonight.''

Jenna looked around at the beautiful furniture and smiled. ''Well, I suppose I can force myself to—'' which was as far as she got before Ian had her on his bed, stripped of her clothes and wrapped around him.

Their coming together was explosive and quick. When Ian could get his breath back, he said, ''You were saying?''

''Was I?'' she said lazily. ''I don't recall.''

''Good.'' He gave her a lingering kiss. ''I love you, Jenna. You can't imagine how much.''

She smiled sleepily at him. ''I'm willing to allow you the rest of the night to convince me.''

The next morning Jenna awoke to Ian's so-very-light kisses on her eyelids, cheeks, nose, jawline and ear. Her body had already responded to his caresses and she had turned toward him, entangling her legs with his.

She opened her eyes sleepily and murmured, ''Good morning.''

His mouth was mere inches away from hers when she spoke. With an innocence she didn't believe for a second, he replied, ''Oh! Did I wake you?''

She rolled her eyes and grinned at him. ''You think?''

He pulled her closer, their bodies plastered together, his face in her hair. He held her that way for the longest time, until she had almost drifted off to sleep again, before he spoke.

"Would you have accepted Chris's job offer, do you think?"

She stretched and said, "Who knows? I might have."

"Not if I had any say in the matter, I assure you."

"Speaking of Chris, what did he think of the contract?"

"He said I shouldn't hesitate about signing once he's spoken to their legal department regarding a few changes. I've been doing a great deal of thinking about all of this and I've come to some decisions regarding how I want to spend the rest of my life."

Jenna replied, "Married, I hope."

He kissed her. "Absolutely. Marriage is a given. No, this is about my career. I've never told you what I do, have I?"

"Nothing specific, no. Your career has been rather mysterious, actually."

"That's because what I do is highly classified."

"Oh. Well, if it's classified…" her voice trailed off.

"I work for the Security Service, the U.K.'s civilian intelligence agency."

She pulled away from him. "You're a spy?"

He attempted not to smile, but failed in the attempt. "A field operative."

"Isn't that dangerous?"

He sobered. "It can be."

"And that's what you'll be doing when you return to London next week?" she asked, horrified.

"If I go back."

"If?"

"While discussing the contract with Chris the other day, I faced the fact that I've really enjoyed being here and writing. I'm not certain I want to go back to being an operative. I never thought I'd say that, but my priorities are shifting."

"If I get a vote in your decision, I sincerely hope you write full-time."

"I plan to discuss this with Todd when I go into the office on Monday."

"You're Philip, the spy in your book, aren't you? All the things he did—you've done them, haven't you? No wonder your scenes are so realistic."

"I wrote about what I know."

"You were actually on that yacht the night everything went wrong for him?"

Ian replied, "I didn't write about any of the operations I've been a part of. They're classified. I do have an active imagination, you know," and he proceeded to show her exactly how innovative he could be until they were both gasping for breath.

Sometime later, Ian said, "When I saw your sisters yesterday I had a glimpse of our possible future…having a family, living here with you and spending our time together. That's when I recognized the opportunity being offered to me. I have the means—with the contract—to stay here and write full-time, chase you around the desk, interrupt you when you're working—that sort of thing—or continue to risk my neck. The answer is obvious.''

''You weren't injured in an auto accident, were you?''

''No, but that's more than I'm supposed to say. The official word is that I was in a pileup on one of the main arteries going into London.''

''Oh, Ian,'' she whispered, her voice shaking. ''Please don't let anything happen to you.''

''Todd won't be happy with my decision, but from the questions he asked about my writing I have a hunch he won't be all that surprised.''

She leaped on top of him, kissing him over and over. ''Thank you, thank you, thank you! I'll do my best to keep you from getting bored with your ordinary life and yearning for your days of dangerous living.''

''Oh, I have no doubt about that.''

Two weeks later

''Ian? This is Greg.''

Ian leaned back in his desk chair with the phone to his ear. ''Good morning. I know we've been remiss about getting back over there....''

''Don't worry about it. That's not why I called. I wanted to let you know I've spoken to Douglas Gordon by phone. When I told him who I was and why I was calling, the poor guy became quite emotional.

The triplets are definitely his. He's been under the impression for all these years that they died with their mother.''

"Well, what do you know? Your hunch paid off, Greg. Congratulations.''

"I've arranged for us to meet him tomorrow. I hope that fits with your schedule. He sounded so anxious to see them, that I hated to put him off any longer than absolutely necessary.''

"Nothing in my schedule is more important than this meeting, Greg. Where do you want us to meet?''

"There's a pub in Oban.'' He gave the name and address. "Let's hook up there at one o'clock. Sir Douglas said he would send a car to pick us up and take us to his place. He'd wanted to see his girls, as he called them, as soon as we spoke but I convinced him that tomorrow would be the earliest we could get there.''

"We'll be there. Now I've got to break the news to Jenna and stop her from tearing over there right now.''

Greg laughed. "I know what you mean. I'm glad Nick's here to help me keep these two calm. We don't want any premature births around here.''

Ian chuckled and hung up. He knew exactly where to find Jenna to give her the news.

The gardens.

After all these years, Jenna thought as she and Ian drove to Oban the next day, my childhood dream of having a family has come true. I have a father. She had been adjusting to meeting him ever since Ian had told her about today's appointment.

Now it was little more than two hours before she would see him for the first time. She wondered what he looked like, what sort of personality he had. Ian had assured her that her father was as eager to meet her and her sisters as she was to meet him.

She didn't believe that could be possible.

Once they arrived in Oban, she was too nervous to eat more than a few bites. Ian had worked hard to keep her calm, she knew. He frowned when he looked at her plate.

She was used to his frowns and ignored them. Besides, she knew he was concerned about her and was touched.

Her sisters and their husbands had already been at the pub when they'd arrived. Seeing them had brought tears to her eyes. She'd hugged her weepy sisters and hadn't missed the exchange between the men.

"You'll get used it," Nick said to Ian, watching the three women now. "If you think it's bad now, wait until she's pregnant. I've learned to carry extra handkerchiefs wherever we go."

"I'll admit I've never seen her quite so emotional. Jenna is generally unflappable."

Greg said, "So is Fiona."

"So I'm supposed to believe that Kelly is the only one with overactive tear ducts?" Nick asked

The men laughed. "Not at all," Greg said. "This is an emotional time for them. I'd be more surprised if they weren't showing how they felt."

"Jenna's a little nervous about this meeting. She still remembers her aunt Morwenna's reaction to her."

Greg replied, "She needn't worry." He turned to the women. "I doubt Sir Douglas slept at all last night," he said to them. "To catch you up on what I've learned about him, he told me that he found Moira's grave in Craigmor months after the attack—even with only her first name he recognized that the day she died was during the time when he was in the hospital in critical condition. Eventually he remarried." He smiled at the women. "Not only have you found each other, but you have two half brothers, as well. Sir Douglas mentioned that both of them are at school in Edinburgh. He said he barely survived his brother's attack. By the time he was aware of his surroundings he discovered that Moira had disappeared and his brother had been arrested. His father was the one who actually saved him by finding him moments after the attack happened. He made certain that his younger son was properly punished."

"What a mess," Ian muttered.

"There was no way to find out if Moira had died before or after giving birth," Greg continued.

"Even if the MacDonalds heard about his inquiries regarding triplets perhaps being born there, it's my belief they probably thought he was the evil uncle looking to destroy the babies. Eventually he was forced to give up his search and assume the babies had died, as well."

"Poor man," Nick muttered. "No wonder he's so eager to see them now. Discovering they're alive and they want to meet him would seem like a miracle, I'm sure."

When the driver walked into the pub, he immediately recognized the three women and came directly to the table.

"Sir Douglas sent me to pick you up." He smiled. "This is a very big day for the Gordon clan, let me tell you. If you're ready to go, we'll be on our way."

Jenna's eyes widened when she saw the luxurious touring car. Once inside, no one spoke. They were too engrossed in the surrounding scenery to say anything. The car followed the curving road, which revealed the sea and an island near the coast.

The massive stone structure on the island reminded Jenna of Ian's castle. Both appeared very old and yet well cared for. When the driver slowed and turned onto the stone bridge that connected the island to the mainland, Jenna realized that this place must be where her father lived.

The thought seemed strange, considering where and how she grew up.

The car stopped in the curving driveway in front of a massive entrance door. Ian helped her out of the car and wrapped his arm firmly around her, wordlessly giving her comfort and his support.

Fiona and Kelly stood and looked around them in awe, before the three of them shared a wordless look of wonder.

A manservant opened the door and welcomed them into the great hall. The walls were covered with an arsenal of spears and other ancient weapons arranged in geometric circles. An enormous fireplace covered most of the rear wall of the hall.

Jenna was awed by the sheer magnificence of the place. Before she could get a grip on her emotions, double doors opened on one side of the hall, revealing a tall, silver-haired gentleman, standing militarily straight.

"Please," he said quietly, "come in." They followed him into a long room where furniture had been grouped into sitting areas. He turned and stared at each one of the triplets. He seemed somewhat shaken when he said, motioning to chairs nearby, "Please make yourselves comfortable. May I offer some refreshments?"

All of them quickly demurred. Once seated, the three couples looked at Douglas. Jenna felt too tongue-tied to think of anything coherent to say.

Greg introduced himself to Douglas as the man who had first contacted him. Then he introduced each of the others. Although Douglas politely acknowledged the men, his eyes kept returning to the three women, murmuring each name as he looked at them one by one.

Finally, he said, his voice gruff with emotion, "Thank you for coming today. There is no way I can adequately express what it means to me to know that you survived, after all. If I'd ever seen any you I would have known immediately that you were Moira's child. The resemblance is striking."

Kelly said, "I don't know if Greg mentioned the fact that only Fiona grew up in Scotland."

"I didn't know."

"I was adopted by a couple from New York and Jenna moved to Australia at an early age with her adopted parents. It's only been the last few months that we knew we'd been adopted and that the other two existed. Finding you has been wonderful since we were told that you had died a few days before our mother."

Greg said, "The attorney told me that it was Moira's wish to have her babies adopted separately so that your brother wouldn't find them."

Douglas nodded, his flexing jaw the only sign of his emotional state. "I cannot express enough how sorry I am that you never knew your mother. How she would have loved to see the three of you now."

"She thought you were dead," Kelly said. "According to the solicitor, Dr. MacDonald said that Moira didn't want to live without you."

"I understand her feelings, believe me." Douglas

took out his handkerchief and wiped his face. "I wish my sons were here to meet you. That will come later, I hope."

"Is your wife here?" Fiona asked.

Douglas smiled wryly. "My wife divorced me some years back. She said she was tired of competing with a ghost."

"You loved our mother very much," Jenna said, speaking for the first time. She'd been moved by her father's obvious love for her mother.

"Yes, very much. There were times when I wished that I hadn't survived the attack, I felt her loss so keenly."

Jenna rose and walked to where Douglas was seated. "Well, you have the three of us now, Father. I'm so glad we found you."

As though released of all restraints, the other two sisters gathered around him, all talking at once. Ian looked at Nick and Greg and nodded toward the door. The three men slipped out to the hallway and quietly closed the door behind them.

Nick shook his head sadly. "The poor man will probably drown in all the tears that are being shed over him." Greg laughed.

Inside the room, Fiona asked Douglas, "Would you mind telling us more about our mother...and you? How you met and fell in love. How long you were together, that sort of thing."

For the first time since they had arrived, Douglas smiled. Jenna could immediately see why her mother would fall in love with him. More than twenty-five years later, she found him to be an attractive, virile man.

"I was a pilot in the RAF when we met. I was in London on leave when I first met her. A friend of mine was dating a friend of hers and they introduced us.

"By the end of the evening I was totally enamored. She kept whatever she felt about me to herself, so that by the next day I was pestering my buddy to help me find out what she thought of me. She told me later that she'd fought not to be impressed by me, and we both laughed about that.

"We laughed a great deal whenever we were together. Once I returned to the base, we kept in touch by phone and letters. When I was released from my duties and ready to return home, I asked her to marry me." He paused, looking from one to the other before adding, "She refused."

"She refused!" the three echoed in disbelief. "Why?"

"Oh, she had some silly idea about being a secretary and my being the heir to an ancient holding. I insisted on bringing her home to meet my family. Thankfully, they fell in love with her, as well.

"She got pregnant right away and when we found out she was carrying triplets the entire family rejoiced...except for my brother, I'm afraid. Not that any of us knew at that time how much he resented my return home and the fact that most of the family holdings would be going to me.

"The night of the argument, he told me how he'd wished that while I was gone I'd die in some training accident. He sneered at my marriage to someone he felt was beneath us socially and told me how much he'd hated me all his life. When he suddenly attacked me with the fireplace poker, I was caught off guard, never dreaming he'd follow his words with such violence.

"He was drunk, you see, and I had long ago learned to ignore his ramblings, but his rage was something new and I wasn't prepared. My father told me that Moira must have seen at least part of that because she left, taking our car.

"Because I was losing so much blood, my father called for an ambulance as well as the constable and had my brother arrested, something my brother never expected our father would do.

"When the constable had his men out looking for Moira, the weather was really bad that night, all they found was our auto in a ditch. They surmised that she was given a ride but they lost her trail. She must have gone into labor soon afterward, because she died less than a week after I was attacked."

The story had reduced all three women to tears, which they furiously tried to hide.

"I know how painful it is to talk about that night," Jenna said. "Thank you for letting us know.

No one knew who she was or who you were because she refused to give them your name.''

Fiona spoke up. ''I understand that my adopted father, who delivered us, heard her mutter your name over and over as her fever climbed and he told his solicitor. Otherwise, we'd never have known anything at all about you.''

They were silent, thinking about what he had just shared with them. Finally, Douglas said, ''We can't change the past, so we must enjoy every moment of the present. I believe that Moira knows we've found each other. I wouldn't be at all surprised if she helped the process along.''

''Like my finding my adoptions papers after all these years,'' Kelly said.

''And Greg's search leading him to me,'' Fiona added. ''He kept saying that he was guided onto my lane the night he found me, but since he was running a fever at the time, I put his mutterings down to his high fever.''

''I don't know why I felt such a strong urge to come here from Australia and leave everyone I knew,'' Jenna said thoughtfully. ''At the time I thought it was to find my relatives in Cornwall. The encounter in Cornwall led me to Scotland. What were the chances of being seen by someone who thought I was Fiona. I wouldn't be surprised if Moira *did* have a hand in our reunion.''

Douglas stood. ''Well, now that you're here, I hope you'll stay overnight and give us a few more hours to share stories. I'm very interested in how each of you found your charming husbands.''

"Oh, Ian and I aren't married," Jenna said hastily. "We're engaged. I certainly understand Moira's hesitancy about marrying one of the landed gentry. I'm a secretary while Ian is a MacGowan. I never expected when I went to work for him that I'd be marrying him someday!"

As they walked to the door to find the men, Douglas said, "Then our stories have come full circle." He opened the door. "I think it's time for me to get better acquainted with my new sons-in-law."

During dinner that night, Douglas said, "Ian, I've spoken with Jenna and she tells me that you're in the process of planning your wedding. Since I wasn't able to attend the wedding of Fiona and Kelly, I'm hoping you'll allow me to host the wedding and reception here."

"Whatever Jenna wants," he replied.

"He's a goner," Nick said, laughing. "Listen to him, already. The poor guy doesn't stand a chance."

Greg said, "Watch it, Nick. Kelly is giving you 'that look.'"

Nick picked up Kelly's hand and kissed it. "Yes, dear?" he asked meekly, causing the rest of them to laugh.

Jenna had never looked so happy, Ian thought, smiling as she joined in the teasing. Content? Yes. In love? He certainly hoped so. Happy about finding family at last? Definitely. This meeting today was the culmination of all her hopes and dreams.

As an only child, Ian had never given much thought to the importance of family until Jenna appeared in his life. Now he was discovering that perhaps he'd missed out on a great deal by not having siblings. He had a feeling that his new sisters- and brothers-in-law would change that.

He reached for Jenna's hand, content to have her within arm's reach.

Chapter Eighteen

"Oh, Jenna," Fiona whispered. "You look exactly like Moira in that dress. Like a fairy princess."

"Why shouldn't she?" Kelly said. "It's Moira's dress. Dad had the oil portrait painted from her wedding photograph."

Jenna stood before a three-way mirror upstairs in one of the many bedrooms of the Gordon home, staring at the image before her. She didn't look like herself at all. Her hair was covered with a pearl-studded cap that hid her reddish-blond hair. Moira's hair had been fiery red, more like Fiona's.

The underskirt of the gown was made of satin, the overskirt lace covered with seed pearls. Age had turned the white lace to ivory.

Jenna had been amazed to find that the dress fit her perfectly. "I feel like a fairy princess," Jenna replied. "I'm so pleased Dad kept the dress all these years."

"Do you ever think what it would have been like for the three of us to have been brought up together in this house?" Fiona asked wistfully. "If we had, I would never have known my parents or you, yours," she said to Kelly. She looked back at Jenna. "It's so sad you didn't have yours growing up."

"I learned a long time ago that it was a waste of my time to lament over things I can't change. I'm so grateful to be standing here in my mother's beautiful wedding gown, my sisters attending me, my own true love waiting downstairs to marry me. The present is much too wonderful to waste any energy looking back."

Kelly spoke up. "I can't believe you insisted I be one of your attendants." She made a face. "I look like a barge. No one will be able to see around me to glimpse the bride."

"I'm quickly catching up to you in size," Fiona pointed out. "This is what we do for our sister."

Kelly sighed. "Oh, don't mind me. I'm feeling grumpy this morning."

Jenna and Fiona looked at her. "Are you feeling all right?" they asked in unison.

Kelly waved her hand. "It's nothing new, I assure you. I can't remember the last time I was able to sleep more than half an hour at a time. Poor Nick gets kicked in the ribs whenever I try to lie next to him. Do you have any idea how long it's been since I saw my toes? I have to take other people's word that they're still there."

"What do you think of Ian's parents, Jenna?" Fiona asked, no doubt hoping to distract Kelly.

"I couldn't believe how cordial and friendly they were to me. His mother, especially, seems absolutely thrilled that he's finally getting married. She said she'd despaired of ever having grandchildren."

"How does Ian feel about that?" Kelly asked.

"He wants a family, as I do. He said he would leave the timing to me, that he just wants me to be happy."

"Talk about having the man wrapped around your finger!" Kelly said.

Jenna laughed. "I fully expect him to turn back into the gruff, grumpy and growly man I first went to work for as soon as the wedding vows are spoken."

"Of course you do. And you appear terrified by the prospect."

"Well," Jenna said modestly, "I do have my ways of getting him into a better mood."

The three of them laughed.

There was a tap on the door. Fiona walked over and opened it. Kevin, their fifteen-year-old half brother said, "It's time, ladies. Dad sent me up here to tell you." He saw Jenna and said, "Wow! You look exactly like the portrait in the den. It's spooky. Are you sure you aren't a ghost?''

''Positive,'' Jenna replied. ''Do you want to touch me to make certain I'm real?''

Kevin turned red and hurried away.

Jenna found her father waiting outside the closed doors to the sitting room, which had been turned into a rather lovely chapel. He wore the Gordon plaid and looked like a regal Scottish laird.

Tears stood in his blue eyes when she joined him. ''You look just like her, you know.''

''I consider that to be the highest compliment I could receive. It's such a privilege to wear her gown. Thank you for offering it.''

Douglas wiped his eyes and faced the closed doors. Nodding at fourteen-year-old Kyle, his other son, to open the doors, Douglas waited with Jenna as first Fiona, then Kelly, entered the room to the strains of ''The Wedding March'' being played by the organist.

When it was their turn, Douglas patted her hand. ''Here I've only known you for a few weeks and I'm already giving you away,'' he said gruffly, leaning to kiss her cheek.

''Oh, you won't get rid of me that easily. You'll probably get tired of my popping in so frequently.''

With the back of his hand he brushed the cheek he'd kissed. ''No, dear, that will never happen.''

Ian hated crowds. Almost as much as ties. It was a toss-up, actually. He particularly disliked crowds that were all staring at him. Chris stood beside him, looking relaxed and more than a little amused by Ian's nervousness.

He wasn't nervous because he was getting married. He'd been counting the days. He would have much preferred, however, to have participated in a private ceremony with only the two of them and the pastor there.

Instead, the room was filled to capacity, every folding chair occupied, all waiting to see him make a complete fool of himself.

Or so it seemed to him.

He glanced at his father, who winked. He glanced at his mother, who gave him a teary smile, and he glanced at Nick and Greg, who sat in the back row where no one else could see them, silently laughing at him, their arms folded comfortably over their chests, as though he were participating in some kind of initiation ritual that they had also experienced and survived.

He'd already heard how much they'd disliked going through all of this. Their advice to him had been to give up and give in to whatever the women wanted. It would save time, since he'd lose any argument he attempted against the three of them.

The doors opened and Fiona walked in. Her dress was masterfully made, hiding her advancing pregnancy. She walked toward Ian lightly and gracefully, her smile radiant.

Chris leaned over and whispered, "Just my luck. Three of them and you grabbed the last available one. There's no justice in this world."

Ian ignored him. He didn't care what anyone said to him today except for Jenna agreeing to marry him.

He hid his smile when Kelly walked in. All three women were petite. At the moment Kelly looked like a delicate tugboat coming toward him. No amount of fashion design could hide the fact that she was very pregnant.

When she drew closer, he smiled and winked at her. She looked startled, then grinned infectiously in return.

And then…Jenna appeared and he forgot anyone else was in the room. She looked tiny standing beside her tall father. He'd heard about the dress and had seen the painting, but this was the first time he saw Jenna's uncanny resemblance to the woman in the painting.

She looked exquisite.

Ian waited impatiently for her to reach his side. Once there, she handed her bouquet to Kelly and faced the pastor.

Ian had no idea what either of them said as they repeated their vows. It didn't matter. He was finally marrying the love of his life.

During the reception, Nick wandered over to him and asked, "Made plans for your honeymoon?"

Ian lifted his brow. "You mean I actually get some say in that decision? That's good to know."

Nick laughed. "I checked with the others, and since we hadn't heard of any plans, we decided to offer you these."

He handed Ian an envelope. Ian looked at it, feeling its bulk. Puzzled, he opened it and stared in bewilderment at the contents he'd removed. Finally, he looked at Nick and said, "Tahiti?"

"Kelly and I honeymooned there. I think you'll enjoy it, as well. It's a long flight and I booked you first-class so you'd be as comfortable as possible." He lifted a brochure from Ian's hand. "This is the hotel. They have secluded bungalows so you don't have to see anyone if you prefer to be alone. Go, enjoy and come back with deep tans."

"I don't know what to say," Ian said. "You shouldn't have spent—"

"Uh-uh, we don't talk about money in this family. We enjoy it, that's all. I'm happy to do it. You both deserve the very best and I—"

"Nick?" Greg said, "Sorry to interrupt but Kelly needs you."

Nick stiffened. Sounding alarmed, he asked, "What's wrong?"

"Nothing to worry about," Greg casually replied. "I think she's in labor. From the little experience I have, I'd say she's been having contractions for some time because she seems to be having bearing-down ones now."

"What!" Nick spun around, scanning the room. "Where is she?" he asked, a note of panic in his voice.

"Douglas happened to be standing with her when she suddenly gasped and almost went to her knees with a contraction. He sent me to find you while he put her in your bedroom and called the doctor."

Nick raced to the door without another word.

Ian looked at Greg, who nonchalantly sipped his drink and gazed around the room.

"Bearing-down pains?" Ian repeated in surprise. "Surely not so soon into labor."

Greg looked back at Ian. "Naw, they're still contractions. I just enjoy seeing the coolly inscrutable Dominic Chakaris shook up a little. He'll find out soon enough that we'll be here for the long haul." He looked around the reception hall. "The wedding guests, at least those who want to stay, will be able to greet the newest arrival to the Gordon clan."

Ian was still concerned about Greg's cavalier way of treating the expectant father. "Remind me never to believe you in an emergency."

Greg sobered. "Actually, you can, Ian. Nick and I are there for either of you. Now that we married a female version of The Three Musketeers, I figure we're going to need to stick together to survive!"

As it turned out, Karyn Nicole Chakaris obligingly arrived in plenty of time for her aunt and uncle to greet her and still make their flight that evening.

Mother and daughter were fine, although Ian was a little concerned about Nick. The expectant father must have suffered every labor pain Kelly did and was on the verge of collapsing when Ian and Jenna said their goodbyes to the family.

Ian couldn't help but wonder how he would manage in a similar situation. Probably not as well as Nick had.

The remaining guests waved them off after Jenna and Ian had changed into clothes more appropriate for traveling. On the way to the airport, Ian said, "Do you realize that we're going to be flying during our wedding night?" Ian lamented, half-seriously.

Jenna grinned. "I'll do my best to keep you from getting too bored."

Ian leaned toward her and gave her a brief kiss before returning his attention to the road. "I'm counting on it."

* * * * *

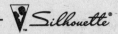

SPECIAL EDITION™

Secret Sisters...

Separated at birth—in mortal danger.
Three sisters find each other and
the men they were destined to love.

International bestselling author

Annette Broadrick

brings you three heartrending stories
of discovery and love.

MAN IN THE MIST
(Silhouette Special Edition #1576)
On sale November 2003

TOO TOUGH TO TAME
(Silhouette Special Edition #1581)
On sale December 2003

MacGOWAN MEETS HIS MATCH
(Silhouette Special Edition #1586)
On sale January 2004

Available at your favorite retail outlet.

If you enjoyed what you just read,
then we've got an offer you can't resist!

Take 2 bestselling love stories FREE!

Plus get a FREE surprise gift!

SPECIAL EDITION™

Available in February 2004 from bestselling author

Allison Leigh

A brand-new book in her popular
TURNABOUT series

SECRETLY MARRIED

(Silhouette Special Edition #1591)

Delaney Townsend was an expert at dealing with
everyone's problems but her own. How else could
she explain that the whirlwind marriage she thought
had ended definitely hadn't? Seems her supposed
ex-husband, Samson Vega, had refused to sign the
official papers. And the more time Delaney spent
with Sam, the more she wondered if the only
mistake about their marriage was ending it....

Available at your favorite retail outlet.

COMING NEXT MONTH